Dear Romance Reader,

Welcome to a world of breathtaking passion and
never-ending romance.

Welcome to *Precious Gem Romances*.

It is our pleasure to present *Precious Gem Romances*, a
wonderful new line of romance books by some of America's best-loved authors. Let these thrilling historical
and contemporary romances sweep you away to far-off
times and places in stories that will dazzle your senses
and melt your heart.

Sparkling with joy, laughter, and love, each *Precious
Gem Romance* glows with all the passion and excitement
you expect from the very best in romance. Offered at
a great affordable price, these books are an irresistible
value—and an essential addition to your romance collection. Tender love stories you will want to read again
and again, *Precious Gem Romances* are books you will
treasure forever.

Look for fabulous new *Precious Gem Romances* each
month—available only at Wal★Mart.

Lynn Brown, Publisher

D1559732

HOME TO STAY

VELLA MUNN

Zebra Books
Kensington Publishing Corp.
http://www.zebrabooks.com

ZEBRA BOOKS are published by

Kensington Publishing Corp.
850 Third Avenue
New York, NY 10022

First Printing: February, 1999
10 9 8 7 6 5 4 3 2 1

Printed in the United States of America

To the Over The Hill Gang

ONE

I want to be with him. Only him!

Brent Roy's first, last, and nearly only words echoed inside Kristen Childers as she drove through Roswell, New Mexico. The twelve year old was in no position to order anyone to do anything. However, *he* might be Brent's salvation and the answer to her dilemma. Might, she reminded herself. First came a lot of work on her part.

Well, she'd jumped through hoops in order to place kids in foster homes before. The only difference this time was that Brent Roy was half Mescalero Apache, and she was heading toward a construction site at the south end of town because that's where his uncle, a full-blooded Apache, worked.

Joe Red Shadow. The name had an intriguing ring to it. A man to go with that name would be hard-honed and mysterious, physical. She easily imagined him dressed in a breechcloth, a war-painted horse under him, eyes narrowed against the sun as he scanned his wild world.

After a day filled with danger and courageous deeds, he'd come home to a woman who understood and shared his ties to the land. They'd walk out onto the desert as the sun set, listening to nature's sounds, the human voices low and intimate. They'd come together as the wind played its ageless tune and the newborn moon looked down on them. They'd make love in that ageless and primitive place, hearts and bodies—

Sucking in a deep breath of air, she fought the heat in her cheeks. How could she indulge in erotic fantasies about a man she hadn't yet met, a man she needed only one thing from? Joe Red Shadow was a potential foster parent and she, a social worker. And a grown woman who knew all too well that what went on inside a man's mind was a lot more important than how he looked.

As the construction site came into view, thoughts of what she and Red Shadow needed to discuss faded from her mind and she gave herself up to absorbing impressions. Brent hadn't been sure what his uncle was building, just that it was beyond the city limits and big. Big was right. So far, the structures consisted of foundations and frames, one of the metal skeletons extending three stories into the clean New Mexico sky.

So Joe Red Shadow worked for the company or corporation or whatever it was that was behind the motel/convention center that was Roswell's latest economic shot in the arm. The site was alive with workers, many swarming over what there was of the buildings. Others drove heavy machinery, massive tires kicking up a fine curtain of dust. The site appeared chaotic and fragmented, but somewhere at the core of all this activity must be a grand plan, men who knew exactly what they were doing, and why.

Feeling out of place, she closed the car door behind her. Wishing she looked like anything except what she was—a bureaucratic employee in a world of muscles and strength—she looked around. Some of the workers gave her no more than a glance, while others studied her openly.

They've got you pegged; get used to it.

It occurred to her that she'd have the best chance of being directed to Mr. Red Shadow if she went to the trailer set up near a graveled parking area. Not only was it the sole permanent structure, but two trucks bearing signs that read MESCALERO APACHE CONSTRUCTION were parked there.

"Ya lookin' for someone?"

She turned and faced the man who'd spoken. His face, a weathered landscape of lines, reminded her of a dry creek. He wasn't much taller than her five foot six but carried at least another fifty pounds, most of them muscle.

"I hope so," she said. "I need to talk to a Joe Red Shadow. I understand he works here."

"Work? Ya might say that. What ya want him for?"

Taken aback, she regrouped behind a momentary silence. Then she spoke. "Is he here?"

"Yeah, but he's busy as hell. If ya wanna leave a message, I'll have him call ya."

The truth was, she'd like nothing more than to finish her business here and get back to where she belonged, but that wasn't possible. She told the sweating, middle-aged man that what she had to say wouldn't take long, hoping that would get him to point her in the right direction.

"I guess," he muttered. "He's been here since dawn. Probably won't git home 'til midnight, without no more interruptions, that is."

So she was an interruption. Noting the almost frantic activity, she was inclined to agree. Unfortunately, Mr. Red Shadow wasn't the only one with a job to do. Concentrating on hers, she repeated her request. After grunting, the man whirled and stalked away. Taking that as an invitation to follow, she divided her attention between his back and the fat cables coiling over the ground. Heat prickled the back of her neck; instinct warned her that more than the August weather was responsible for the crawly feeling. She was still being evaluated.

Her reluctant guide stopped at the base of what was going to be a three story structure. "Shadow!" he yelled. "Ya got company."

"Later," someone yelled back from above. "I'm busy."

"That's what I tried to tell her. She won't listen."

"Damn!"

At first she was able to make out little except for the building's solid frame. Finally though, she detected movement and followed a man's progress as he descended from the uppermost steel beams. There wasn't any kind of a ladder that she could see. Rather, he had somehow found boot and finger holds in the unfinished structure, his movements smooth and practiced.

He was shirtless. Dark. Big, strong. Muscular. Even more alive and potent than he'd been in her imagination.

Reaching what she took to be the separation between the second and bottom story, he balanced effortlessly as he made his way along a six inch wide beam to a vertical steel column. Catapulting himself from the structure while still four feet off the ground, he spun toward her. Power. Everything about him radiated it.

"What do you want?"

"You—you're Joe Red Shadow?" *Stupid question.*

"Yeah. What do you want?"

"I—I need to talk to you about your nephew."

"Brent? What's she done now?"

"She?"

"My sister, Brent's mother. Are you a cop?"

"No," she told him, aware that she should be introducing herself as a member of the Children, Youth, and Family Department, here to talk to a relative about the welfare of a twelve year old boy who could no longer live with his parents, or parent, as was the case with Brent.

But this man had gleaming black eyes that looked as if they'd been alive for a thousand years, and she felt herself being pulled back through those years with him. His shirtless body had been carved and formed by physical labor, making him not beautiful but compelling. Nearly six feet tall, his rocklike shoulders and arms were capable of transforming barren ground into a manmade marvel. He might be part of today, but his eyes were of the ages, challenging her to take that journey with him. A word, a touch, the wind singing for and to them and she'd—

"No," she managed. "I'm not a cop. I'm a social worker."

"Hm. Give it to me straight and fast. What happened?"

Clearly Joe Red Shadow wasn't a man who knew the meaning of indecision. She easily imagined him facing everything life threw at him. Still, she wasn't sure how to begin. When he breathed, the effort began deep inside him and expanded until everything about the broad and dark chest was involved. Sweat glistened off smooth flesh pulled taut over solid muscle. A small black and white feather was fastened to a slender leather thong around his neck. He probably didn't notice it gliding over his flesh, but if it were her hand instead . . . she stopped her wayward train of thought and concentrated on answering him.

"Your, ah, your sister's been arrested," she said, shocked by her flustered tone and the image responsible for it. Swallowing, she tried again. "And she's not being allowed bail."

"Damn. What'd she do?" He swore under his breath.

"Apparently she tried to rob a convenience store. An employee triggered an alarm and the police were able to pick her up because her car had broken down. Ah, she had a knife. That might be added to the charges."

"Where was Brent?"

"With her. I guess he tried to run, too. All I got was secondhand information from the officer who took Brent to the emergency shelter."

"Have you seen him? How is he?"

"Quiet," she said, warmed by the concern in his voice. "I—he might be in shock. Watching your mother being arrested is a traumatic thing for a boy to experience."

"It isn't the first time, lady. She never should have— Was she drunk?"

"It looks like it," she said, in part because she'd seen Hannah Roy and in part because her brother's eyes told her he wouldn't allow anything less than the truth.

"So my sister's in jail and Brent's at an emergency shelter. What's your name?"

She told him. His nod was nearly imperceptible. "At

least she didn't hurt anyone," she hurried to reassure him. "But you're right. This isn't the first time she's been in trouble. I imagine that's why she's been refused bail."

"They'll probably throw away the key," he muttered. "All her screwing up has finally caught up with her."

"The reason I'm here is that Brent can't stay where he is. Because he's Indian, the tribal council is involved. They asked us to do the preliminary work, but they'll be making the final decision." She slid her hand under her hair and pulled it away from her neck in an attempt to cool herself. "The Mescalero tribal council wants him placed with one of his people."

Something changed inside the man. She could almost reach out and touch the protective curtain he'd wrapped around himself. "No," was all he said.

"No?"

"I can't take him."

I want to be with him. Only him. Brent's words, spoken in defiance and desperation, reverberated inside her and made her angry. "Why not?"

"It doesn't matter."

Doesn't matter! "He wants you. *You.*"

Pain. If she lived to be a hundred, she would never change her mind about the emotion that had just slammed into him. With the raw frame of a massive structure behind him and the sound of monster machinery vibrating around them, he looked capable of handling everything life threw at him, except hearing that a twelve year old boy needed him.

"That's what your job's about, isn't it?" he challenged. "Finding places for kids whose mothers are flushing their lives down the toilet."

"That's part of it. But Mr. Shadow, I—"

"Joe. Call me Joe."

Joe. Strong and concise, honest. "All right. He doesn't want to go to the reservation, which is what the council will dictate if there's nothing in Roswell that meets their criteria. He says he's never lived there. He'd be out of his element. He needs someone who cares, familiar surroundings."

The man now reminded her of an animal trying to find his way out of a cage. Although his body remained motionless, his jaw clenched and those unbelievably expressive eyes became even darker, even deeper. Energy coming from a source beyond her comprehension radiated out from him and made him seem larger somehow, even more complex.

"What is it?" she asked. "Brent told me he hasn't seen his father for years. He also said your mother is dead and although your father lives on the reservation, he isn't well. I got the impression there's only you and your sister but maybe there's some other relative?"

"No. There isn't."

Joe. Joe, you're all he has. "Is there something about Brent you're not telling me?" she pressed. "Maybe—maybe you have young children you don't want him around?"

"No." The word was spoken slowly, his voice more growl than whisper. "That isn't it."

"Then what—"

"I'm not good for him, lady."

"Not good?"

He nodded, once.

"I don't . . ."

Why was she doing this? If Joe wanted nothing to

do with his nephew, she should begin the difficult task of finding a nurturing home for Brent to live in. But she couldn't ignore what was going on inside this hard man with the eagle feather slowly rising and falling on his naked chest, couldn't pull herself free from the silent and dark battle taking place inside him.

"No," she said with a calm that belied everything she felt. "I don't get it."

He blinked. She would have concentrated on that except the wind was running through his long, ebony hair and he'd pulled his hands into fists that transformed his forearms into stone. A part of her shrank from his power. Still, she was fascinated.

"I can't help that, lady." He spoke slowly, a man barely holding in something that wanted out. "My reasons are just that, mine. Brent's better off without me."

"Why?"

"You wouldn't be asking if you knew—look, this project is my responsibility. Mine." He indicated their surroundings. "It's my neck on the line. My signature on the loans. I don't have time to look after Brent. Hell, I barely have time to sleep."

"Your responsibility?" she repeated.

"My construction company. This is the biggest project I've ever taken on. I've got more than thirty men and women working for me, and right now I can't think of anything else."

If she'd known that, she wouldn't have pushed him and might not have come out here in the first place. But that's not what he'd said a minute ago. *I'm no good for him* had been his exact words.

"Can you at least tell Brent that?" She was goading him when she had no business doing so, but those dark eyes held a challenge she felt compelled to take on.

"Tell him what?"

"That your business commitments make it impossible for you to devote enough time to him." How professional she sounded, how bureaucratic.

"Look, lady." He leaned toward her. "I don't know what else I have to say before you get it. It isn't going to work. Understand, it isn't going to work."

Because you won't let it. Because you've boarded yourself up. "Fine." She sounded angry because she was, that, and intimidated. "Play it your way."

"I'm playing it the only way I can."

Without saying another word, not even whether he was going to get in touch with his nephew, Joe spun on his well-worn boots and stalked away. He headed toward a massive piece of earthmoving equipment, legs and back and shoulders meshing together until his movement was so smooth and fluid that it took her breath away.

His ancestors had been warriors. They'd fought the invasion of their land and won a reputation as fearless fighters. Today's Apaches retained much of their heritage, many of them living on the mountainous Mescalero Apache Indian Reservation one hundred miles to the west. The Mescaleros ran their own ski resort as well as ranching and lumbering concerns. He had every right to be proud of what he was accomplishing here, but if that commitment was so all-consuming that it left no room for his nephew's needs—

Shaking herself free of her thoughts, she looked around, but before she could take a step, her attention was drawn to Joe, who was talking to whoever was driving the piece of machinery. Head tipped back, one leg lifted so he could rest his boot on the equipment. From where she stood, she couldn't see his face, was spared having to look into those incredible eyes.

Still, she couldn't stop herself from taking in his wide back, bunched muscles, glistening skin. Did his body feel the effects of his already long day, or were his reserves of strength so great that he could continue endlessly?

Maybe, like the warrior of her earlier daydream, he'd never run out of energy, always be ready for moonlit desert walks with the woman he loved.

TWO

Night had claimed Roswell by the time Joe Red Shadow let himself into his house. He closed the door behind him and leaned against it before commanding his legs to take him into his office. Only then did he flip the switch that put an end to darkness. A quick glance told him that two faxes had come in and the answering machine was blinking. Ignoring them, he opened his window. The fan over his desk brought a cooling breeze against his flesh.

Stripping down to his briefs, he started for the bathroom but stopped near the photograph on the wall behind his desk. Breathing deeply, he studied the dark-eyed girl's face, seeing himself in the high cheekbones and square jaw. He needed to take his clothes to the washing machine, but his body felt spent. It was easier to stand with the moving air on him.

Resolutely taking his eyes off his daughter April's picture, he turned to the willow and devil's-claw basket resting on his bookshelf. He picked it up, marveling at the artistic quality of the timeless handiwork. Predominantly light brown, black devil's-claw fibers had been used for the decoration which depicted horses and deer. It had been given to him at his mother's death, a gift from an elderly woman with gnarled hands and knowing eyes.

"Take it wherever you go," Alice Swift-Runner had told him. "As long as you have a piece of what it is to be Apache, you can touch your heritage."

That's why, although he'd been offered a thousand dollars for the basket, he would never give it up. Proof of who and what he was, like the yucca "wood that sings" or Apache fiddle in his bedroom and his passion for Native American rodeos—things that helped keep him sane.

He was thinking too much when nothing except showering and eating should matter, but Brent wanted to live with him. His nephew hadn't made his request in person because he was buried somewhere within the social service system. Instead, the young woman had come.

With his brain exhausted, he couldn't remember the social worker's name, but her voice was low and faintly husky, like a breeze touching prairie grass. Her hazel eyes were flecked with green that danced when sunlight touched them. He didn't think she'd put much effort into her makeup which he preferred to the model-perfect look. Her dark brown hair was short, probably for practicality, although allowing it to fall around her face might soften the image she presented to the world. He wondered if the effect was deliberate

She was maybe five foot five, and because she was slender, he'd been able to tell a great deal about her bone structure and was impressed by what he saw. Like a lean filly, she was strong and healthy, quietly secure in the way her body functioned. Even if she'd been aware of his scrutiny, he doubted she'd have guessed why her smooth-muscled arms had made more of an impact on him than her full breasts. The explanation was simple; he lived in a physical world; success or failure in that world depended on what a physique was capable of accomplishing.

He guessed she spent most of her time behind a desk which meant her brain was her most important tool. Still, she handled herself with an innate grace that would hold her in good stead if she ever stepped into his world, if he ever allowed her to glimpse what that world meant to him.

It didn't matter, damn it. He had no reason to see the serious woman with the probing yet private eyes again, no need or desire to risk the wall he'd placed around himself being penetrated.

The shower helped revive him, as did dinner. He read the faxes and debated returning the phone calls, but in the end convinced himself that it was too late. His sister was in jail, again. Acknowledging that brought his thoughts back to Brent's social worker, and this time her name easily came to him. Kristen Childers.

She shouldn't have pressured him. Shouldn't she have looked into his background before asking him to take responsibility for his nephew? If she had, she wouldn't have approached him and he wouldn't be struggling with—

There was no struggling to it; there wasn't! He'd told her the truth when he said he was no good for Brent. Why couldn't she accept that fact and leave him alone? Only, he acknowledged, as he turned on his computer, it wasn't just she who had followed him home tonight. It was also his love for Brent, his conscience—his something.

The screen lit up. He pulled out the folder of interviews he'd conducted on the reservation last winter and tried to put his mind to the task that often robbed him of sleep but left him with a deep sense of accomplishment. Tonight, however, he couldn't concentrate.

Instead, he wondered what her reaction would be if Kristen Childers could see what he was working on. Would she understand why he felt compelled to record the ancient legends and stories before the old ones died and with them their wisdom and the ties to history?

What would her reaction be if he told her about his personal journey to this point in his life? Strangely, he wanted to tell her so she would understand why his heritage meant so much to him, but if he did, he would have to reveal the mistakes he'd made, soul-deep regrets, and he couldn't do that. He wouldn't allow her any closer than she'd already gotten.

Instead, he'd work through his insomnia by compiling the book that represented his people's heritage. He wouldn't let images of a graceful, dark-haired young woman distract him.

Liar, he thought.

"Any luck?"

"I'm afraid not."

"You put everything to him?" Kristen's supervisor asked as he lowered himself into the unoccupied chair in her small office. "He knows how few options his nephew has?"

Although she resented Bob Cogswell's tone, she reminded herself that the man talked to everyone the same way. "He knows. He's in charge of the construction going on at the convention complex and says he has no time for the boy."

"Maybe. What's his home life like? Any chance his wife could take responsibility?"

A wife? "Bob, I'm not going to push a child on someone who doesn't want him."

"So you're giving up?"

"Of course not, but I don't have that many options. That's why I was hoping Joe . . . Joe." There was that name again. Wasn't it bad enough that it and the man himself had dominated her dreams, taken her thoughts into the desert where fantasy waited?

"I'm going to contact him again today," she said, once she'd pulled her unwanted emotions back under control. "He's had time to sleep on it. Maybe he's changed his mind."

"It's not going to happen," Bob grumbled as he got to his feet. "Mark my words, this boy is headed for trouble if things don't turn around for him in a hurry."

Kristen waited until Bob had left before pressing her hand to her forehead. What really bothered her was that Bob was right. Without a mix of love and discipline and guidance, Brent could wind up in detention, or worse. Somehow she had to try to make Joe understand that.

She was looking through a case file for the phone number at the construction site when her intercom buzzed and she was told she had a call from a Joe Red Shadow. Feeling as if time had slowed somehow, she watched herself push the appropriate button, heard herself say hello.

"Mrs. Childers?" Dense and low, his voice wound itself around her. "We need to talk."

"All right." Her cheeks felt hot and words were unexpectedly hard to come up with.

"Not during the day. I don't have the time."

"It would be hard for me too," she said. The truth was, she didn't want to see him until she'd had time to prepare, even if she didn't know what she was preparing herself for.

"What about six?" he asked. "I think I can cut myself loose by then."

"Six?"

"You don't work after five?"

"It's not that." She should be accustomed to his tone by now, but it continued to vibrate through her. "It's my daughter. I don't want her to have to stay at day care."

"Daughter?" He took a deep, slow breath. "Okay, bring her along then."

"Ah, all right," she finally agreed, then named a restaurant halfway between where they worked. If he was aware that she'd chosen a very public place, so be it.

"Will you tell me what you want to talk about?" she asked.

"Not now."

Joe Red Shadow dominated his surroundings, making Kristen wonder whether he did it deliberately, or if he was oblivious of his impact on people. Although five year old Susanna continued to chatter about what she wanted for dinner, Kristen noted interrupted conversations and lingering female looks as Joe made his way to her. She couldn't say he flowed because there was too much substance and muscle to him for that. Rather, he reminded her of a well-tuned athlete, a unity of all the separate parts into a smooth-running whole. If he'd been born an animal, he'd be a panther.

When he stood before her, she realized he was waiting for permission to sit. The truth was, she wanted to jump to her feet and run from the challenge and danger and excitement of him. Still, she was a civilized woman concerned with the welfare of one of her clients, and that was what made it possible for her to politely indicate the chair across from her. As Joe sat, Susanna pressed herself against her.

"This is my daughter," she told Joe. "She's a little shy." Shy didn't begin to touch what Susanna was going through, but that was none of this man's business.

Joe acknowledged Susanna with a smile and a nod. She would like to believe Joe understood Susanna needed time to take her measure of him, but most likely he couldn't care less that his nephew's social worker had a child. To keep silence from taking over, she said it had been hot but the breeze had helped. He nodded, then explained that when wind gusts hit over thirty miles an hour, he ordered his employees to work on the ground. She admitted she'd never thought about that. His tone resigned, he told her that in his business, the weather could never be ignored. If she hadn't been careful, she might have made the mistake of telling him she couldn't imagine him ever not being aware of his surroundings.

When the waitress arrived, Kristen ordered for herself and Susanna. Joe asked for a plate of nachos to be served while waiting for their meal.

"I didn't have time for lunch," he said by way of explanation, then downed his water in three quick gulps. "Or enough water," he added. "Have you been waiting long?"

"We just got here." In the artificial light, his eyes reminded her of polished obsidian. His hair all but glistened, making her wonder if he'd taken a shower before meeting her. "As usual, I didn't get away as soon as I wanted to," she belatedly finished.

He grunted and after holding her gaze for so long that she'd begun to feel trapped, he glanced at Susanna. The waitress had given Susanna a page from a coloring book and crayons, and she was busy sorting through the crayons. Either she was intrigued by having her favorite thing to do or was using it as an excuse to ignore Joe. Kristen guessed it was a little of both.

Taking advantage of Joe's interest in what her daughter was doing, Kristen gave him what she hoped was a casual perusal. His jeans were identical to the ones he'd worn yesterday except that this pair had a small snag at the right hip. His white cotton shirt, although unironed, was clean. For a moment she fantasized that he'd dressed just for her, but she didn't want a man to be that interested in her. Especially not this one, with that air of something primitive and hotly alive clinging to him. Pulling herself up short, she noticed that Joe was still watching Susanna.

"She'll be busy until dinner arrives and even longer unless I make her put her drawing away," she said in an effort to jump-start the conversation again. "Art is her passion."

"Good. Everyone needs something to feel passionate about."

Yes, oh yes. "And—and your obsession is buildings?"

To her surprise, he shook his head but said nothing as the waitress delivered his nachos. Joe popped a cheese-laden corn chip into his mouth. He sighed. "Wonderful. I was so hungry I could have eaten nails."

At that, Susanna looked up and regarded Joe with a skeptical and yet fascinated expression. "I was just kidding," he told her. "Nails would break my teeth, wouldn't they?"

Susanna nodded, then, her cheeks flushed, she returned to her coloring.

"Well," Kristen said when silence hung between them. "I guess we should discuss . . ."

Joe pushed his plate to one side and rested his elbows on the table. For the briefest of seconds, she thought only of the generations of black-eyed, black-haired Apaches who came before him. Even if he had on a suit and tie, he would be a man for the out-of-doors. She'd never thought about whether certain people weren't designed to live surrounded by walls, but it was obvious when it came to Joe Red Shadow.

"What's been going on with Brent?" he asked, the question pulling her back to reality. "You said he was running out of time at the shelter home."

"We can probably argue for a few more days," she explained, the social worker in her kicking in, "not that it's going to make much difference."

"Why?"

Piped-in music had begun to play, a drum's steady beat making an impact on her senses. She wanted to move with the sound, to concentrate on the rhythm. Most of all, she didn't want to be aware of Joe Red Shadow any more, or maybe the truth was, she wanted man and music to merge.

Gathering herself, she told him there was a shortage of foster homes and even if there wasn't, the tribal council didn't want Brent isolated from his heritage.

Joe took another bite without taking his eyes off her.

"I'm sorry if this isn't what you want to hear," she finished. "But it's what I have to deal with."

"Rules."

"Rules," she agreed, smiling at the realization that they were on the same wavelength in this regard. "There's no getting around them, is there?"

"No, there isn't." He sounded resigned. Then: "I'll take him."

"You—what made you change your mind?"

What indeed, Joe asked himself. He could have told her the truth, at least as much as he understood, but the words might reveal too much about who and what he was.

"I did," he said. "Isn't that enough?"

Her look plainly said he hadn't come close. He tried to concentrate on how he was going to deflect that, but it wasn't easy. Her eyes kept changing colors, one moment green, the next a shadowy hazel. When her daughter had looked at him, it had been with identical eyes. They carried the same wariness, the mother's tinted with wisdom, the daughter's clinging to innocence.

He knew that quality. His daughter's eyes had it too.

"Yesterday," Kristen said, pulling him back to the reason for their meeting, "I believe you had no room in your life for Brent. What brought about this change?"

The restaurant was too crowded and noisy. The drumbeat in the piped-in music intrigued him, but he couldn't concentrate on it. Kristen Childers was sitting too close, smelling faintly of some kind of flowers, her fingers resting easily on the tabletop. "I've had time to rethink things."

"Have you? Maybe your wife had something to do with your decision. She—"

"I'm not married."

She studied him without blinking, but he couldn't imagine what was on her mind.

"My sister raised Brent by herself. There's no reason I can't do the same."

He waited for her to point out that Hannah had done a lousy job of parenting, but she didn't. "I know," she said with a glance at her daughter.

"Then what's your objection?"

She nibbled on her lower lip, something his nervous system didn't need. "It's not an objection, Mr. Re—Joe. But you said you didn't have small children around when I asked if that's why you were hesitant to take Brent. Maybe you don't have much experience with them."

Not as much as I wish I did. "At times he and my sister lived with me," he said. "I know what he likes to eat, the kind of clothes he wears, that he's good in math but his writing skills are poor. He loves country and western music and he wants a pickup when he's old enough to drive. What else do you need to know about him?"

He could tell by the way she leaned back that she'd taken his question as a challenge, but couldn't decide whether he wanted to change her impression or not. For the first time since the two of them started talking, he felt as if he had the upper hand.

Or maybe the truth was, things were happening that he had no control over, but it didn't matter because Brent's welfare came first. This woman had somehow found a place in his life when he didn't need and couldn't handle any more complications.

THREE

"I have the feeling you don't want to talk about why you changed your mind," Kristen said after their meal had been served. "However, I'm going to have to know more."

He'd known that was coming. Still, he needed time to reconcile the direct words with her soft femininity. Everything between them would have been easier if sexual attraction hadn't entered the mix, at least on his part. He had no way of tapping into what her reaction to him might be.

"I can't detail everything that went into the decision," he said. "This is best for Brent. Is he aware that you were going to talk to me?"

"Yes." She fixed him with a gaze that seemed capable of reaching through any barrier he might try to erect. "And he told me again you're the only one he wants to live with."

"I see."

"Joe, my job is to make life the best it can be for the kids I deal with."

"It's even more so with me when it comes to my nephew." His tone was fierce. Not caring what she might make of his directness, he went on. "I've been worried about Brent for a long time, but my sister loves her son—at least as much as she's capable of. I didn't want to jeopardize their relationship."

"And now you feel it's your responsibility to—"

"Not my responsibility! I want him."

His outburst caused Susanna to look up in alarm. "I believe I have something to offer my nephew," he continued in a softer tone. "I'd like to be given the chance." *Besides, I love him. You're a parent; you should understand.*

"I don't have the final say. I hope you realize that."

She'd been getting close with her words, making him forget her official role in this, but what she had just said brought things back into focus. He didn't dare forget her power over him.

"Why don't you lay it out to me?" He didn't try to keep the challenge out of his voice.

Kristen did, but because she'd already told him about the role the tribal council played in approving the placement, he didn't learn anything new, found no way of defusing the resentment that came from being forced to deal with a massive social system. Instead, he concentrated on her expressions and the way her voice sounded both soft and strong. She worked at keeping her emotions to herself; he saw that in the way she kept her head and hands still, the beautiful eyes that wouldn't allow him beneath their surface. He pondered how much might be drawn out of her at the right time and place, by the right man. By him.

"What happens now?" he asked. "Does Brent have to stay where he is until I've been checked out?"

"No." She glanced at her daughter, then resumed her steady gaze on him. "After he's with you on what we'll call a temporary basis, I'll conduct a home study.

Once the council has that information, it's possible they'll identify other concerns I'll need to address."

He didn't like that her "observations" carried so much weight any more than he liked knowing she would be invading his personal space. "When can I have him?" he asked, surprised by how many conflicting emotions she'd evoked in him.

"Maybe as soon as tomorrow. It depends on how long the paperwork takes."

"Good." He straightened, his muscles tight but ready as always. "I'll be ready."

"I hope so."

"What do you mean?"

"Just that there are so many aspects to be considered, things that could go wrong."

"You're making it sound as if we're on opposite sides of the fence."

"I—social workers learn not to take people at face value, Joe."

He wanted to know whether she mourned not being able to trust her fellow human beings, whether that lesson had been learned solely on the job or if some of it had come from her own life experiences. Most of all, he needed to ask himself why he cared.

"Life 101," he said with a short, mirthless laugh.

"Life 101." Again she glanced at her daughter, her features instantly gentle. The air hummed and sparkled with the love Kristen Childers felt for her child. Because he wished he was looking at his own daughter tonight, he threw up the old, scarred defenses that kept him sane. April was happy with her mother. Marci was a good and loving parent.

"Look." His tone was businesslike, almost harsh. "I need you to be honest with me about everything. If you have reservations or questions or concerns, come to me. Don't go behind my back."

"I hope I won't have to."

He didn't want this! Damn it, he was having dinner with an intelligent, attractive woman. Tonight should be for getting to know each other, for the tentative dance of a man and a woman exploring the possibilities of a relationship. Instead, he was closing down, protecting himself.

"And I don't have the time or inclination to play games," he added. "An employee steals from me and he's out of a job. I hear rumors that someone's questioning the way I do something and I go to that person. Do you know what I'm saying?"

"Oh yes, I do."

"Good."

She sighed and looked a little off balance. "If I feel I have to confront—"

"Confront? Does it have to be adversarial?"

Although she said nothing, he swore he could hear the wheels turning in her head. Everything about the restaurant felt artificial. He didn't want plastic plants and cartoon figures on the walls. He wanted the quiet and peace and naturalness of the reservation where his father lived, wanted Kristen Childers exploring it with him.

"This is my first experience with your agency," he admitted. "I don't know what to expect."

"Each situation is different," she said with a short nod. "I'd like to tell you that most times things work out to everyone's benefit, but no matter what you want, I have to put the children I'm responsible for first. Providing for their well-being is why the agency exists."

"Do you like what you do?"

"What?"

"I asked—"

"I know what you said," she interrupted. "But what I think of my job has nothing to do with what you and I are discussing."

"I disagree." His tone, he thought, was adamant, not sharp or confrontational but judging by the way she'd leaned away from him, maybe he was wrong. The little girl also had a wary way about her, and he winked at her again. "Understanding where you're coming from will give me a better idea of what kind of a relationship we'll have," he said. "If you're a by-the-books person, its going to be quite different than if you allow your emotions to rule you."

"Mr. Red Shadow, I'm not the one under scrutiny here. You are."

"And if I don't like it?"

Susanna had been cutting her sandwich into very small pieces. But at his outburst, her hands stilled and she looked from him to her mother and back to him again, her eyes big.

"How's your meal?" he asked in a deliberate attempt to get her to relax—and maybe learn more about the mother through the child. "Whenever I make myself a cheese sandwich, I have to dip it in ketchup."

"Ketchup?"

"Sure. But it's funny." He worked up a confused expression. "I love Mexican food, but I've never put ketchup on it. Do you think it would taste better that way?"

Susanna's nose wrinkled and he couldn't suppress

a smile. Sensing Kristen's eyes on him, he returned her gaze. She had that mother lion look.

Picking up the paper Susanna had been coloring earlier, he pretended to give it his full attention while keeping his emotional antenna tuned to Kristen. "What's that?" He pointed at the drawing in the lower right hand corner.

"A horse," she said tentatively.

"You like horses, do you?"

"I *love* them," the little girl said eagerly.

"So do I," he told her. Then he explained that his father had been a ranch foreman when he was a boy, and he'd been given responsibility for grooming and exercising the horses. Some of the mother lion look went out of Kristen's eyes, but he had no doubt that she was absorbing every nuance of his behavior. He asked Susanna if she'd ridden many horses. She shook her head.

"I want her initial experience to be a positive one," Kristen explained. "It'd be easier if I knew someone with a gentle, older horse."

Susanna nodded agreement. "Not a rodeo horse," she said emphatically.

"Why not?"

" 'Cause they bunk off the cowboys."

"Buck," Kristen corrected. "They buck."

"I don't care. They're mean."

"No, they aren't," he told her. The urge to hug the child was strong. "I've ridden in many rodeos, and I've never met a horse I was afraid of. Those who buck just don't like being ridden."

Susanna straightened, her eyes wide. "Have they bunk—bucked you off?"

"Lots of times."

"Wow! You have to be really brave to do that, don't you?"

"Either that or dumb."

Was this her daughter, Kristen thought as Susanna asked Joe if he knew how to draw horses and surrendered her paper so he could demonstrate. True, her experience with men was limited, but that wasn't the only reason Susanna usually lapsed into silence when around adult members of the opposite sex. Chalk that up to her ex-husband Cliff who had no idea how to be a father and made her doubt her ability to judge the worth of any male. But children were perceptive, and if her daughter had sensed something good about Joe Red Shadow—

What did it matter? She and Joe had only one thing in common, only one reason to have anything to do with each other. When that had been resolved, they'd go their separate ways and she'd no longer have to battle her unwanted responses to him.

"Do you think he's ever afraid?"

Pulled out of her thoughts by the question, Kristen glanced at her daughter. Susanna still clutched Joe's impressive sketch of a rearing horse, long mane and tail flowing.

"Afraid?"

"Of being hurt. He's been throwed lots of times."

Kristen contemplated correcting her daughter's English, then let it go. In truth, she had to fight to concentrate on anything. She couldn't remember if she'd said anything to Joe about when she'd be getting back in touch with him and didn't think he'd brought it up either. Instead, he'd spent most of his time talking to Susanna, twice reducing her to helpless laughter as he told her about foals who chewed on their mothers' tails, their disapproving snorts the first time someone put a saddle on their backs.

Joe, who'd given Kristen the impression he hadn't spent much time around young children, knew exactly how to reach beyond a five year old girl's reserve and into that child's world. And he'd left his impression on her mother as well. Left her hungry in a way food could never touch.

Reminding herself of Susanna's question, she said she believed everyone was afraid when they did something with the potential to be dangerous. However, different people had different ways of handling that fear.

"He wouldn't cry if he got hurt, would he?"

"Grown-ups don't usually cry about things like that, honey."

Susanna frowned but didn't ask why, which Kristen appreciated. True, she could tell her daughter that emotional pain hurt more than any cut or bruise, but she didn't want to be sad tonight. Whether she was seeking distraction or giving into impulse, she didn't know. Either way, she rolled down the window to let in the night's smells and breeze, selected an easy-listening radio station, and lost herself in the experience.

Joe Red Shadow was essentially gentle—for which she was grateful. Where Cliff's fists and voice had led him through life, Joe's eyes said the most about him. They were quiet and dark, and seemed deeply connected to his soul somehow . . . a soul she wanted to know.

She didn't want to think about Joe's body but want-

ing and reality had nothing to do with each other tonight. It was as if his physical form had a love affair
with life. Whatever experience came his way would be
not just accepted but embraced.

Did he take to lovemaking in the same way?

And why couldn't she silence the questions?

After pulling into the drive of the emergency foster
home the next day, Kristen turned off her car. Just
then she heard a vehicle behind her. Glancing in the
rearview mirror, she recognized Joe's truck. She sat
where she was, content and anticipating, uneasy, alive.
He had on his work uniform of snug, worn jeans, cotton shirt open at the throat, and boots. He'd obviously
driven here with the windows open. As a result, his
hair tangled around his head and she couldn't prevent
the word "wild" from dominating her impression of
him.

Last night they'd talked about the tone of the relationship that had to exist between them. She had no
doubt that he was uncomfortable not being in control
of any situation, but they were concerned with a boy's
future, not steel and wood and cement or riding a
rodeo animal.

That's all there was between them—a boy in need
of a home, a man willing to provide that, and a woman
with the means and responsibility for making it come
about.

Nothing else existed.

"Brent knows I'm coming?" Joe asked when she
joined him in walking to the front steps.

He was too close to her. Either that or her nerve
endings were too sensitive. Breathing took concentra-

tion, and yet she couldn't pull away. Being near him awakened the woman in her, and she didn't want the experience to end.

"Yes," she finally answered.

"Hm. Has he said anything to you about what he's been going through?"

She told him she was trying to get Brent into counseling to help him deal with his mother's arrest and everything that had gone before it.

"That's not what I asked. Have *you* talked to him?"

Instead of answering, she pressed the doorbell, silently counting down to the end of the dangerous seconds of it being just the two of them. As they waited, their bodies too close together, she explained that she'd tried to talk to Brent, but he'd refused to respond. The only thing he seemed to care about was that he live with his uncle.

Joe said nothing, and yet she detected a subtle change in him. His body, strong and straight, softened as if stirred by some emotion. His fingers hung easy at his sides, and he'd cocked his head slightly to the side, making her wonder what he was thinking. If things were different between them, maybe she could ask for access into those thoughts.

After the house father invited them inside and went to get Brent, she leaned against a wall while Joe stood in the middle of the room, his presence dominating both the space and her emotions. Just the same, she told him that the tribal council had given tentative permission for Brent to be placed with him. The final approval would take longer and might include certain contingencies.

"Contingencies?"

Trying to dismiss the wariness in Joe's voice, she

explained that the council would at the very least want her report. They might request a financial statement from Joe, letters of recommendation, assurance that he remain in close contact with Brent's school. "They'll probably stipulate that Brent spend some time on the reservation."

"They don't have to worry about him knowing what it is to be Apache. I wouldn't have it any other way."

Before she could ask him to be more specific, Brent entered the room. Joe stepped forward in that fluid way of his, erasing the distance between himself and his nephew. He held out his hand and when Brent placed his smaller one in his, Joe pulled Brent close.

"You've grown," Joe said, his voice rough.

"Yeah. I have."

Silence stretched out, but Kristen sensed that neither of them was uncomfortable with it. Brent, who often avoided eye contact with her, stared up at his uncle. Joe responded to the unspoken communication by returning the gaze, his body deeply, richly alert. For a second, she surrendered to that hunger she couldn't explain but screamed to be acknowledged. She wanted Joe to give her that much of himself, to feel wanted and needed—loved.

"I wish you'd called," Joe was saying. "If I'd known—"

"I didn't know what to tell you."

"No." Joe's tone became thoughtful. "I don't suppose you did. Brent, I understand what kind of person your mother is. There don't have to be any secrets between us."

Brent nodded but didn't say anything. She prayed that Joe Red Shadow would turn out to be what Brent needed, but sensed on some instinctive level that she was looking at the answer.

His words halting and passionate at the same time, Brent told Joe everything that had led up to this moment. Joe kept his hand on the boy's shoulder.

"When can I see my mom?" Brent asked.

"I don't know," Joe said. "You'll have to ask Mrs. Childers."

She wanted to tell both Joe and Brent that the legal system, not her, controlled Brent's mother's fate but doubted that either of them was in a mood to listen.

"Why does she do the things she does?" Brent muttered after she'd explained that she'd contact the district attorney's office about visitation. "Some of it is so crazy. Sometimes, I swear, it's like she's trying to self-destruct like a video-game character or something."

"She isn't doing it deliberately."

"I know it. I'm glad she got caught."

"Why?" Joe asked, his eyes leaving Brent to lock with Kristen's. She felt for a moment as if she'd been allowed a glimpse into the man's heart.

"Because now my mom can't pretend she hasn't made a mess of everything. Uncle Joe, do you think she'll ever get her act together?"

"I don't know," Joe said. His body language fairly shouted that nothing and no one mattered to him except what he and his nephew were talking about. A fierce thankfulness surged through her—that and something else she struggled to deny. "I'd like to believe she will," Joe continued, "but my sister's had a lot of years and opportunities to turn things around and she hasn't."

"You did," Brent said.

"It was different for me."

"But why," Brent challenged. "You were wild. Mom says you were and I know . . ."

"You know what?" Kristen pressed. A faint alarm had gone off inside her when she'd heard the word 'wild'.

"Nothing," Brent muttered. "It doesn't matter."

But it did. "Joe, if there's something I should know—"

"There isn't. Brent, why don't you get your things."

Brent nodded and said it would only take a minute to grab his belongings. She waited until the boy was gone, then spoke. "What was Brent talking about?"

"It's the past. What does it matter?"

"Matter? You told me you believed in the direct approach. I asked a question. I deserve an answer."

"In other words, you believe you have a right to probe every aspect of my life."

I don't want to. I want it to come willingly from you, for you to want to share— "I'm sorry you feel that way, but I wouldn't be doing my job if I didn't ask."

"Your job! It feels more like a club you're holding over me. Either I play the game your way or you take Brent from me."

"Look, I—I realize you resent my role in this situation, but I don't have a choice."

"Didn't you ever resent authority, Mrs. Childers?" he asked, the question coming from deep inside him. "Or maybe you were a good little girl who never questioned anything."

"This isn't about me," she blurted. "The only thing that matters is whether you're the right person to be responsible for Brent."

"I am."

Sunlight had been streaming in the front window when they first came into the room but now that was being filtered by a cloud. Joe's features had become indistinct, shadow and shade instead of reality. She fought the powerful and unfathomable desire to sink into darkness with him, to absorb the darkness that she sensed was a part of him.

"Did you hear what I said?" Joe asked, his words shaking her free, if not from his impact at least from the insanity of it. "I'm the only person for Brent."

Neither of them was in a position to debate that, but instead of saying so, she absorbed the intensity in his voice and made it part of her growing understanding of him. Joe Red Shadow might once have been an untamed young man; some of that quality still clung to him. But he'd embraced and been embraced by responsibility and faced his obligations head-on.

What would it feel like to have those powerful emotions directed at her?

FOUR

Kristen hadn't heard from the tribal council by the time she reached Joe's house early Friday morning. She'd have to arrange for a thorough home study with Joe and Brent, but the first days of a new placement were critical and often set the tone for the long run. At least getting a first impression was her official reason for dropping by his place on her way to work, and if she'd taken a little more care than usual with her appearance, there was nothing to be read into that.

Joe had chosen a home with a real feel of the past. She estimated it to be at least forty years old with a massive yard. White stucco, it made a statement about Southwest tradition. The sun-faded tile roof echoed the same message as the hardy mature trees, unmanicured lawn, and gravel driveway. It was one of several widely spaced homes on a long, quiet road, and she found herself longing for that kind of breathing room.

It took concentration and effort to engage the horseshoe door knocker, and although she was slightly disgusted with herself for doing so, she straightened the simple silver chain around her throat and ran a moist tongue over her seldom-applied lipstick while she waited.

Joe, freshly shaven with his hair still damp and his

shirt open, wordlessly let her in. As she stepped past him, a thousand tiny electrical currents sparked; she couldn't remember the last time she'd had that reaction around a man—if ever. A pink blush rose to her cheeks as he explained he'd already made and taken several phone calls which was why he hadn't yet put on his boots.

It shouldn't matter that he was tall even in his socks or that the faint scent of soap and shampoo clung to him and his flat belly eased in and out with every breath, but she couldn't dismiss anything about him. If she'd known he'd look like this or that she'd be so affected, she wouldn't have come.

"If this isn't a convenient time—" she began. "Guess I should have called first."

He shrugged those wonderfully wide and strong shoulders of his. "I was forewarned. You said you wanted to see how Brent and I interact at different times and in different situations."

"Where is he?" she asked. Looking around, she gained an impression not of a bachelor's pad, but of a man's home. The furnishings were spare and well-maintained, tile floor partly covered with handmade rugs, eye-catching paintings and photographs, a predominance of brown and white.

As she took note of a full, built-in bookshelf, Joe explained that Brent was in the bathroom. Leading the way into the small, sunlit kitchen where the aroma of toast waited, he asked if she wanted coffee. Although her nerves needed no more stimulation, she accepted. Their fingers didn't touch as he handed the cup to her, but the promise was there. He was, she discovered, as much in his element moving about a kitchen as bossing construction workers, but then why

shouldn't he be? After all, he was quietly competent
in so many things, and seemed altogether comfortable
in his own skin.

"What about some toast?" he asked as he spread
jelly on his. "Sorry. That's about as sophisticated as
breakfast gets around here."

She wanted to tell him about her and Susanna's
Sunday morning ritual of waffles and strawberries.
She visualized Joe at her kitchen table drinking coffee
while she sliced berries for his breakfast, but didn't
dare ask herself how long it would take for that to
happen.

"So," he said, "I take it this is what's called checking
up on me."

Instantly defensive, Kristen shook her head. "It's
standard procedure, Joe. I know I told you that."

"So you did. And I told you how I feel about having
anyone looking over my shoulder."

She opened her mouth to disagree, but he held up
his broad, competent hand. "I was kind of hard on
you yesterday," he said. "You're just doing your job,
and I can't hold it against you."

"I appreciate that." There were no curtains over
the kitchen window. From what she could tell, there
weren't any close neighbors and the fact that he felt
no need to close himself off from the out-of-doors
didn't surprise her. Her internal electrical currents
had retreated to a low hum, but if she wasn't careful,
they'd go into overload again.

"You look nice," he said.

"I—what?"

"Nice. I don't see many women in dresses. Of
course, given the way I make a living, it's not surpris-
ing."

"Oh? I, ah, most times I don't dress up much."

Feeling off-balance in a way she thought she'd mastered since walking away from her ex-husband, she stalled by sipping her coffee. She found it disconcerting that Joe's hands stilled and his eyes hadn't released hers. She'd just begun to explain that casual dress was the norm, given how much running around social workers did, when the phone rang.

"The answering machine will pick it up," was all he said.

"But if it's business—"

"It's always business."

"You sound as if you resent that."

"Not really, but answering phones isn't high on my list of favorite things to do."

"What is?" she asked, the question escaping before she could stop it.

"You really want to know?"

She could be evasive, tell him it was part of the information she needed to gather, but with sunlight now touching the side of his right cheek and his glistening hair reminding her of midnight, she could only nod.

"Hm. All right. I started doing what I do because I love creating something, love working with my hands." He glanced at his hands, then briefly studied hers. It was all she could do to keep them from shaking.

"I've always been fascinated by building technology," he continued. "But these days I spend most of my time dealing with rules and regulations, bureaucracies."

As he spoke, her attention was drawn to his eyes as she thought of moon-filled nights, great stretches of desert and prairie. His lashes were the same ebony as his hair and spoke proudly, even defiantly, of his heritage. Years in the sun had painted his flesh and forged the fine lines at the corners of his eyes. There was nothing soft or untested about him.

Lovemaking wouldn't change him. Any woman going to bed with him would have to accept his unselfconscious strength, his sure, strong edges. He might try to give that woman gentleness, soft whispers and delicate finger strokes, but the power would always be there.

The sound of Brent's shoes on the tile floor jerked her free of thoughts she had no right thinking. Giving the boy a distracted smile, Kristen told him that his uncle lived between her apartment and where she worked, then asked him about school. From what young Brent volunteered, she surmised that a formal education hadn't been a priority in his life. Although that concerned her, she perceived an innate intelligence in his choice of words and the comments he made about whether today's schools were adequately preparing students for life in the real world.

"Look at it this way," Joe interjected. "No system is perfect. If that's one of the things you're learning at school, you're getting a jump start on the next seventy years."

Brent frowned. "Maybe. But you're the head honcho where you work. You don't have to take orders the way I do."

"Is that what you think? Just follow me around for a few days."

"Does that mean you'll excuse me from classes?"

"Nice try." Joe smiled, slow and gentle and warm. "But the next time you have a break, I'll put you to work."

"Yeah? I want to handle machinery. That'd be awesome."

"You'll work the machines once you've proven you can handle the responsibility, and after you have your driver's license. Your first piece of equipment will be a broom. Clean-up duty."

Brent frowned and took a bite of toast. "Slave driver," he muttered around the wad.

"You better believe it. And you'll be paid minimum wage."

Kristen waited to see if Brent would object. Instead, the boy went to the refrigerator and poured himself a large glass of milk which he downed without stopping to breathe. "You going to drop me off at school or do I have to take the bus?" he asked.

Joe glanced at his watch and winced. "You'd better catch the bus," he said, then pulled out a couple of dollars and gave them to Brent. After assuring the boy that he'd take him to a shoe store tonight, he gave him a quick and easy hug.

Kristen waited until Brent had headed toward his bedroom for his school books. "The state provides a clothing budget for foster children," she said. "I've already authorized—"

"Forget it. I'll buy what he needs, which is just about everything. Brent came to me with almost nothing except the clothes on his back."

He came around the counter and planted himself in front of her, his jeans-clad legs so close she swore she felt his body heat. The electrical currents surged back to life. "If I don't do anything else in this world," he said, "I'll give Brent what he needs to make it."

The passion in Joe's voice hit her low and hard, and

she believed him as she'd seldom believed anything
in life.

"I should have stepped forward long before this,"
he continued. "Why . . ."

Joe's presence and warmth made it nearly impossible for Kristen to concentrate on what he was saying.
She slid off her stool and deliberately turned her back
on him. It wasn't enough; he was still too close, too
all encompassing.

"How does it feel so far?" she asked, her eyes skim-
ming over walls and windows and furniture while her
thoughts remained on the man who'd merged those
things into a home. "Taking in a twelve year old has
to mean major changes in your life."

"No more than what Brent's going through."

After nodding agreement, she wandered through
the living room. If she had been asked to come up
with a one word impression for it, she would have
said . . . light. The walls were white, the windows large.
There was no clutter. All decorating touches spoke of
his Native American heritage and included handmade
baskets, blankets, ceremonial masks, bows and arrows,
even a miniature totem pole representative of North-
west Indian art, not Apache.

Finally her gaze settled on a framed photograph on
top of the bookshelf. Walking over to it, she studied
the dark-eyed girl. With slow realization she accepted
that she'd seen those mesmerizing eyes before—in
Joe. She felt him behind her, felt more than his physical presence. Maybe what reached her was the sound
of his heart beating.

"She's my daughter," he said.

But he'd said he didn't have any children, hadn't

he? No, he had said only that there weren't any children in his house. "Your daughter?"

"She lives with her mother."

Unprepared for the layers of emotion behind Joe's simple words, it was all she could do to keep from embracing him. As a social worker, she should know how to handle this, but she felt lost. Maybe what Joe Red Shadow was feeling at this moment had somehow exposed her reaction to his emotions as well.

"She's beautiful," she whispered. "How old is she?"

"Nearly thirteen."

Wondering if it was wise to find the cause of the love in Joe's voice, she concentrated on simple mathematics. Joe couldn't be any older than thirty, which meant he'd become a father while still a teenager.

"She and her mother Marci are in Albuquerque, next door to Marci's parents," he explained.

"Oh."

"Marci and I owe them a great deal. She was only sixteen when April was born."

Two children having a child. "Are they all right?"

"They?"

"Everyone. Your daughter. Your ex-wife. The grandparents."

"Marci and I were never married."

Stepping alongside her, he picked up the photograph and held it so that the morning light flowed over the girl's features. She would never forget this image of a father looking with love and pride and regret at what little he had of his child. How wrong she'd been to try to label him in any way. He was so much more than an Apache running a construction company, a practical and sometimes hard-nosed businessman, more than the sexiest man she'd ever met.

She should ask for details of his relationship with his daughter because that might tell her more about Joe's ability to provide the guidance Brent needed, but she'd heard Joe's heart beating and knew that what was going on inside him at this moment deserved to remain protected. His alone. At the same time, she knew she'd already seen the size and strength and depth of his love for his daughter and been touched—changed and enriched by that.

Finally he returned the picture to its resting place. He still hadn't buttoned his shirt, but she was only vaguely aware of that. Instead of wanting to run her fingers over his chest, she fought the need to embrace him and in the embrace take a little of his heartbeat for herself.

"Red Shadow?" she managed. "What's the story behind the name?"

With what she knew took incredible effort, he focused on her. "Story?"

"Yes. I mean, it's so different. Fascinating."

"Fascinating? It's tied into our mythology. Red Shadow was the mythical Apache who fathered Fire Hawk."

"Fire Hawk?"

"Think of him as a folk hero. Maybe that'll help you understand his and Red Shadow's role in Apache tradition."

"Why aren't I surprised you're talking about that?" a youthful male voice said, shattering her concentration.

She turned as Brent joined them. The boy slanted a look at his uncle, then faced her. "You want the whole story, the short version, I mean?" Brent asked. "Okay, according to the legends, this Fire Hawk dude who lived about a billion years ago, fought the mountain spirits—whatever they were. When he won, the spirits rewarded him by giving the Apaches the Rocky Mountains which they called the 'Ribs of the Earth.' "

Made uneasy by Brent's mocking tone, she divided her attention between the boy and Joe.

"Can you believe that?" Brent continued. "One Apache supposedly taking on who knows how many spirits and beating them. Like anyone's going to believe that."

"It's legend, Brent." Joe spoke through clenched teeth. "Part of our history."

"Maybe yours, but I don't buy it."

"Not now but you will."

Kristen's first instinct was to defuse whatever was going on between the two. Thanks to her ex-husband, she had an abhorrence of confrontations, but if she stepped between Joe and Brent, she might never understand the breadth and depth and maybe limitations of their relationship and that, she reminded herself, was why she was here this morning.

"If you have your way, I will," Brent muttered.

"What are you saying?" she asked while Joe stared down at his nephew.

"Ask him." Brent pointed a finger at Joe. "He's so hot to force those stupid legends down everyone's throats that he can't think of anything else."

"They're our past, Brent," Joe returned. "Yours and mine. You won't think the way you do now once you understand."

Brent gave Joe a doubtful look. Joe returned his nephew's gaze with narrowed eyes. "This isn't the time for that, Brent," he said. "It took me a long time to appreciate where I came from. I don't want you to have to experience the same rootlessness."

"I'm not rootless. I know exactly who and what I am."

"What are you then?"

The demanding question hung in the summer-scented air. Joe Red Shadow was passionate about the work he did and loved his nephew and daughter, but she'd just discovered another layer to him, one that went deeper than she could have expected. How could she write a concise report when the man remained essentially a mystery—and fascination—to her, when the essence and core of him had yet to be fully revealed?

After a silent moment, Brent muttered that he had to go. Joe put his hand on Brent's shoulder, and although the boy didn't respond, he didn't jerk away either. Once the door had closed behind Brent, Joe walked into the adjacent room and came out carrying a battered briefcase. "I have to leave," he said in that cool, yet warmly sensual way of his. "What else do you need from me?"

I don't know; maybe too much. "Nothing, for now," was all she said.

As Kristen contemplated days and nights with no future contact between them, she couldn't decide whether she was relieved or disappointed. What she did know was that not seeing him wouldn't silence her thoughts, her—did she dare call it need?

"Wait a minute."

Joe's words wound themselves around her as surely as any rope. On edge and keenly alive, she watched as he picked out something on his bookshelf and handed it to her. It turned out to be maybe twenty typewritten pages in a binder.

"If you're interested, read these," he said. "They're Apache tales, what the elders told the next generation so the past wouldn't die."

"So the past wouldn't die. What a wonderful sentiment."

"Yes, it is." He reached out as if to pat the folder. Whether by accident or design, his fingers briefly, too briefly, brushed her knuckles.

You don't feel anything, she told herself as heat and energy laced through her.

The lie died long before the electricity did.

FIVE

"Mommy, what's a wind dancer?"

Kristen blinked and looked at what she'd been reading aloud. The truth was, she couldn't remember what the story had been about. It hadn't been like that when she'd begun the ancient Apache legend, but before long, her thoughts had turned to the man responsible for the pages. Had he worked on transcribing the oral histories late at night or had he risen before dawn? The thought of him wresting time for this from his busy days left her in awe. Obviously it meant a great deal to him, but why? That's what she'd been trying to pull out of the manuscript—that and the essence, the impact of the man.

"A wind dancer sounds wonderful, doesn't it?" Kristen said. "I can't imagine anything more wonderful than being able to dance with the wind."

"But the story isn't about the wind. Do you think that warrior really killed that bear?"

What bear? Warrior? Oh yes, there had been a courageous but mute warrior in the story, along with the maiden he loved. "I'm not sure, honey. Don't forget, these stories are very old. Those things might have really happened, or they might be stories Apache elders told the children, like your favorite movies."

Susanna sighed and wiggled. "I bet Joe Red Shadow knows."

"You like that name, don't you?"

Susanna nodded, then wriggled again. "Do you think he would ever fight a bear?"

Unable to stifle a laugh, Kristen clutched her daughter to her. "There aren't any bears around for him to fight, pumpkin."

"I bet he could do it. Do you think if I called him, he'd tell me what a wind dancer is?"

Her father, whom Susanna called Grandpapa, was the only man the girl relaxed around. That she would consider talking to a man she'd only met once shocked her. "I don't know," she muttered.

"He could 'splain everything, I bet."

"He probably could. Do you really want to call him?" If the phone call was made, it would change the social worker/client relationship. Still, she didn't want to discourage her daughter from reaching out—or cut herself off from the man who'd dominated last night's dreams.

"Maybe tomorrow," Susanna said.

"All right. Maybe tomorrow." Relieved and disappointed because she wouldn't be talking to Joe tonight, she stood and offered her daughter a hand up. They were talking about which nightgown Susanna wanted to wear when the phone rang.

The voice on the other end was masculine and sure, quiet and yet disquieting at the same time. "It's Joe Red Shadow," he said unnecessarily. "I don't mean to call you at home, but I've been thinking and—has your daughter read any of those legends yet?"

"We were going over the first tonight."

"Which one?"

"Ah, I'm not sure of the name. Something—something about a wind dancer."

"Good. That one's safe."

"Safe?"

"There's a couple that are pretty intense. I don't think she's ready for the legend of the black flame. That's a word for Gila monster, but the story isn't about him. Let's just say that when a peaceful tribe is attacked by powerful and vengeful invaders, it gets pretty violent." She heard a voice in the background and told herself it was coming from the TV. The other possibility—that he had a woman with him—wasn't something she could easily accept.

"The thing is," Joe went on, "the way the story starts out, you don't know what you're getting into until it's too late. What does she think of what she's heard so far?"

"I'll let you talk to her," she said. "Hopefully she'll tell you."

Handing Susannna the phone, she studied her daughter's reaction. Although the girl was slow to accept the receiver, she didn't stammer which sometimes happened when she felt threatened. Susanna listened intently and twice the hint of a smile touched her lips.

"A hummingbird!" she explained. "That's awesome."

Whatever Joe said in response made her giggle. Kristen was delighted that Joe and Susanna could laugh and share, but she'd been her daughter's rock, her safety net and protector. She wasn't sure she was ready to have someone else step in, particularly not this man who made her feel unbalanced and alive and sexually aware all at the same time.

Cliff had stripped her of interest in the opposite sex. Her mother worried that the longer she didn't date, the harder it would be for her to enter into a new relationship, but she'd been content to rebuild her self-confidence and concentrate on her daughter and career.

Joe Red Shadow was an unexpected wrinkle, that's all. It wasn't as if she was in heat and even if she was a cold shower would put everything right again—except that she couldn't stop thinking about him or needing more than that too-brief touching of hands.

"All right," Susanna was saying. "If you really want one, I'll do it. Tonight."

"What are you going to do tonight?" she managed to ask.

"Draw Joe a picture of Wind Dancer. He's a very, very, very brave warrior who turned into a humming-bird after the bear killed him."

"Not tonight, honey. You've got to go to bed."

As she suspected, Susanna looked crushed, but after listening to Joe, she smiled and then handed over the phone. Kristen placed it against her ear, feeling connected. She imagined his attention focused on whatever she might say. If there was a woman with him—

"I hope that didn't cause a problem," Joe said, his voice cool and deep and warm all at the same time, just as she remembered. "I didn't say anything about wanting the picture right away."

"That's all right." He had to be alone; she needed him to be alone. "I've learned that for a child, immediate is a lot more interesting than any time in the future."

"She really likes the legends."

"She has trouble distinguishing between reality and fantasy, but I don't think it's going to be a problem."

He shouldn't have called. True, he was glad Susanna hadn't heard about Black Flame, but hearing the mother's voice unsettled him. There was something in her voice that made him think of layers. He wanted to peel away the protective veils she'd wrapped around herself, insanely and recklessly wanted to removed his own layers, but he wouldn't.

"Your daughter's quite an artist," he said.

"She's always loved drawing which is strange because it's never particularly interested me. I don't know where her aptitude comes from."

Susanna had a father as well as a mother. That unknown man had passed on something of himself, not that he was going to be the one to bring that up.

"Oh, I wanted to tell you," she said. "I sent my report to the tribal council, but I'm not satisfied with it."

"What's wrong?"

"Nothing. It's just that it covers a brief period of time, and I really don't know that much about the two of you."

More than I know about you—like what your place says about you and what you wear at night and whether you're sleeping alone, Joe thought.

"Joe? Are you still there?"

"Yeah," was all he could give her.

"Oh. I thought—you didn't say anything."

"I was thinking. Look, it's late. I'd better make sure Brent comes inside."

"Yes. Of course. Joe—"

"What?"

"I just—nothing. Thank you for calling."

He said something and then hung up, but instead of going to look for Brent, he sat staring at the darkened window. Kristen's memory kept coming at him, an essence as illusive as the wind at dawn and just as intriguing. More than anything else, he hated his sense of vulnerability.

"That's all right," Kristen said. "I figured you'd be saying that."

"Did you?" Sam Che, president of the tribal council asked. "I must tell you, several council members still want the boy living on the reservation."

Because Sam had already said that twice since their phone conversation began, Kristen didn't bother assuring him that she understood their position. She hadn't been surprised to hear that the council wanted more than her report. What she wasn't looking forward to was hearing what hoops they wanted her to jump through.

Closing her eyes, she listened as Sam Che detailed the council's concerns. His explanation often digressed into explanations about the personalities of the other council members, how they earned their livings, who they were related to. If she couldn't get Sam to finish up, she was never going to make her next appointment.

"It won't be that complicated, will it?" he asked, pulling her out of her thoughts.

What won't be complicated? "Well," she stalled, "it depends."

"On what?"

Fortunately before she had to admit her ignorance of what they were talking about, Sam launched into an explanation of what he knew about Brent's mother. "Growing up in a chaotic family with all that moving around and her father being unable to hold onto a job, well, I guess it's understandable that she became wild."

That's what Brent had said about his uncle. "It happens," she managed.

"Unfortunately." Sam sighed. "That's why we have to go slow and careful now."

Sam had already said that several times. Hoping to derail him, she assured him that hurrying a placement had never been the agency's way. She also assured him that she'd monitor Joe and Brent as long as necessary. As she did, an image of Joe roped and corralled like a wild horse entered her mind. He was a proud and independent man who was capable of running a large business, but he was being forced to conform to a mind-boggling array of regulations and controls. Although it went against everything she'd been taught in her job, she wanted to cut him free to work out a relationship with Brent.

I'm no good for him. She remembered his words.

"Mr. Che, you're uneasy about this, aren't you?" she asked, a chill snaking down her spine.

"Yes, I am. Brent's mother is facing a prison sentence. I don't want her son getting into a situation that might lead to the same thing happening to him."

Neither did she and that had to matter more than anything else—even her irrational need to release Joe from bureaucratic ropes. She might see him as raw male sensuality, but she didn't dare let that sway her, or ignore the warning her body had just given her.

"There's something we can do." Taking a deep

breath, she forced herself to continue. "I'll have a criminal check run on Red Shadow."

"Good idea. How long will that take?"

I'm sorry. Joe, I'm sorry. "Ah, getting something back from New Mexico law enforcement won't take long, but if he's lived somewhere else, we'll need to make requests to those states as well."

It was so simple, she told herself as she looked over Joe's foster care application. He'd listed both Nevada and California as previous addresses. Depending on the agencies' backlogs, it shouldn't be more than a week or two before she knew a great deal more about the man.

Thanks to a conversation with a friend at the district attorney's office three days later, Kristen learned that Brent's mother had pled guilty to the charges of attempted robbery and assault. Sentencing hadn't been set yet, but given Hannah's previous clashes with the law, she was probably looking at several years in jail. Kristen managed to carve out enough time to drive over to the construction site that afternoon. What had been only the barest outlines of buildings the first time she'd come here had filled out. She felt a wash of sadness that dirt and sand and weeds had been replaced by concrete, then dismissed the thought as she studied the workers, looking for the male form that had never completely left her mind.

Brent, dressed in jeans, boots, and hard hat like the others, was pushing a large broom, occasionally bending over to pick up something which he placed in a bag tied around his waist. From the way the bag sagged, she guessed it was filled with nails, bolts, or screws.

"He's paying you union scale, isn't he?" she asked when she was close enough to be heard.

Brent leaned against his broom and wiped sweat from his forehead. "He better. My skills don't come cheap."

Pleased that he had a sense of humor, she pretended to study his broom. "You don't have to supply your own tools, do you? Something that specialized has to be expensive."

"As long as he doesn't take it out of my paycheck, that's his problem," the boy quipped. "I didn't know you were coming."

"It was either get out of the office or lose my mind," she explained. "Do you know where your uncle is?"

"He's behind you," that deep, dense voice she knew all too well answered.

Heat slammed into her and for a moment she felt too lightheaded to trust herself to move. It wasn't fair! He shouldn't have the power to do this to her!

"Yes." Turning, she looked up at Joe whose eyes were sheltered in the shadow cast by his hard hat. "You are."

His T-shirt—thank heavens he wasn't barechested today—clung to the lines of his flawless body; his jeans looked for all the world as if they were clinging precariously to his hips, and she couldn't dismiss his flat belly, the strength in his denim clad thighs and calves.

"What are you doing here?" he asked.

SIX

Wishing the words weren't so hard to come by, Kristen explained about Hannah's guilty plea. "When something doesn't go to trial, it isn't always easy to learn what happened," she said.

"You mean that's all there is to it?" Brent asked while Joe remained silent.

"She pled guilty," she said. "It's up to the judge to set the sentence."

The boy gripped the broom handle with fingers that immediately turned white and fixed his gaze on Joe. Joe touched Brent's shoulder, and she felt something powerful arc between uncle and nephew. The sounds of men and machines no longer made any impact. Once before Joe had put her in mind of a trapped animal. The same thing was happening now, but why?

"She's done it," Joe muttered. "Flushed her life down the toilet."

"You don't know that," she protested. "Maybe having this happen will result in her straightening herself out."

"Right," Brent hissed.

Kristen said nothing to try to take the edge off Brent's outburst. She was concerned with what the boy was going through, but too much of Joe's emotions reached toward her, and she wondered if she fully understood why he'd looked like a man who'd lost his freedom, or why she so wanted to give it back to him.

Wrenching free of his uncle, Brent began ramming the broom against the ground. She moved as if to stop his furious movements, but Joe stopped her with a warning look, then grabbed her wrist and pulled her with him until they were out of Brent's earshot.

"Let him go," Joe said once they'd stopped. "He's got to let his anger out."

"I know he does. I hated having to do what I did."

Only then did Joe release her. All that remained was the imprint of his fingers on her flesh—and deeper. "Sometimes your job stinks, doesn't it?" he said.

"There are times when I hate it," she admitted, her eyes drawn to the masculine hand that had bound them together. "If I were a secretary or worked in a factory, I could walk away from it at night, but I work with people in crises and sometimes hear and see things . . ."

"Why do you do it?"

His question flowed over her, not disapproving or critical, but almost as if he was spreading a blanket of warmth over her.

"I needed to support Susanna and myself," she admitted. Then before she could judge the wisdom of what she was revealing, the words rushed out. "When I saw what social work paid, all I concentrated on was getting through the application process. I—I'd gone through a rough patch in my life and believed that would help me relate to other people. It does, but . . ."

"Are you going to stay with it?"

"For now, yes."

"Why?"

"Because I happen to believe I can make a positive difference in some people's lives."

"I'm sure you can." His words were still gentle, still accepting. "But I hope you'll know when you've given all you can."

He wanted to take her hand again, but that was all wrong! No matter how much she wanted and needed that, today was about him, not her.

"Joe, maybe I should have told you about your sister first so you could better deal with Brent's reaction."

"Yes, you should have."

Wondering if he was about to criticize her, she tensed and waited as she'd done too many times around her ex-husband, but Joe only rammed his hands in his back pockets. His boots were dusty and something stained his jeans at the hips. The right side of his neck appeared roughened. He needed a haircut and the flesh under his eyes looked smudged. There was nothing pretty about him, nothing soft or civilized.

"I have to ask you something," she said, after giving both of them a few moments of silence and herself a little time in which to try to minimize his impact on her.

"What?"

"How does this make you feel?"

"Feel?"

"Maybe you didn't think you'd have Brent for very long. Maybe knowing your sister won't be able to assume responsibility for him for years makes it hard on you."

Hard? It was funny in a way. Responsibilities snuck up on a person without their knowing the burden was coming until the rope had been thrown. Only there was no rope where Brent was concerned.

"It doesn't matter." The air smelled hot and dry. He wanted to feel surrounded by it, lost in it if only for a little while. Away from Kristen's impact on his senses and emotions. "Making things turn out as good as I can for Brent is all that matters."

"Is it? Joe, when I first told you about your sister, you looked as if you'd been poleaxed. I got the impression you wanted to walk away from the whole thing."

That should serve as a warning of her ability to tap deep into him. Still, despite her instinct or intuition, she hadn't gotten it all right. "I can't tell myself it's all a bad dream any more, that I can't fix what happened to someone I love," he admitted.

"I know."

"Do you?"

"Yes." She met his challenging words with one of her own. "Joe, you aren't the only one who has ever felt as if their life is out of control. It happened to—it happens to most of us."

Suddenly, he wanted to learn everything about when it had been like that for her. They might not have known of each other's existence a few days ago, but life had brought them together and they'd begun to explore each other in ways that went beyond the two children who were part of their lives—at least he wanted to continue the exploration.

"I suppose it does," he acknowledged.

"That doesn't help you; I know it doesn't. No matter what other people have been through, every one of us has to walk alone sometimes."

"My grandparents didn't. They were together nearly sixty years."

"That's—that's wonderful." She sighed and her eyes glistened. "And your parents? Was it the same for them?"

"No. It was hard all the time Hannah and I were growing up. They barely made enough to keep food in our mouths. My father drank and it seemed as if my mother was always sick."

The fingers of her right hand twitched, and in his mind, he felt her small hand settle around his. "You didn't have the support you needed, did you?" She made it, not a question, but a statement. "When you needed guidance, there wasn't any."

The conversation was getting too deep, too tangled when he wanted to swing a hammer until he was so tired he couldn't think. No, that wasn't it. He wanted to make love to Kristen Childers until the world went away. Before he could act on the impulse to pull her into his embrace and cover her soft, feminine mouth with his own, he heard his name being called. Looking around, he spotted one of his foremen gesturing at him.

"I have to get back to work," he told her. He both resented and was grateful for the distraction. "Is there more we need to talk about right now?"

"Yes." She sighed. "I'd like to know how you're handling this."

"Me?"

"Yes, you."

"The important thing is giving Brent the best I can," he told her. "I love my sister. She feels the same about me, at least as much as she's capable of. And Brent means more than anything else in the world to

her, but she's no good to him, or to herself the way
she is now."

"No. I don't imagine she is. Why does that happen?
People want to succeed, but they fail and keep—keep
on failing until others give up. Until those other people have to walk away."

*What's going on here, Kristen? This isn't about Hannah
and me. It's yourself you're talking about, isn't it?* "We all
have powerful instincts for survival," he said instead
of pushing.

"If we didn't, we'd be dead."

It had been that bad? Wondering what Kristen had
gone through, worrying about her, hating whoever
had done this to her pulled him from the complexity
of his own life.

"I'm sorry," she hurried before he could think of
anything to say. "I had no business saying that. Look—
I've got to let the school know what happened to
Brent's mother. I want to get him into some kind of
counseling. If he's burying things inside him—"

"What was it like?"

"What?"

The job be damned. This was more important.
"Your marriage. What was it like?"

She'd kept her hands wrapped around her middle
as they talked. Now, the right one strayed to her throat
and covered it in a protective gesture. Her eyes were
luminous, reminding him of a hurt child. "That's not
what this conversation is about, Joe," she said.

"Maybe not, but that's what I'm making it. Where
is Susanna's father? What happened?"

Her mouth opened and closed. She looked so vul-
nerable standing there. He had triggered memories
of an obviously painful past and if he dared, he would

have embraced her. But what if he did? He'd have to accept her burdens and maybe there wasn't enough of him left for that right now and holding her would be the greatest mistake of his life.

Still, he couldn't stop himself from pushing. "You don't want to discuss him; I understand that, but you're probing into every aspect of my life and—"

"It's my job, Joe."

"I know about your job! But that's not what we're talking about right now."

Kristen could look as trapped as he felt, and yet something kept him going. He didn't understand that force, or maybe the truth was, he wasn't ready to acknowledge it. Everything was so damn complicated when all he wanted to do was breathe.

"Where is he?" he asked. "And don't tell me you don't know who I'm asking about."

"Joe, I—" She glanced at Brent who had stopped his attack on dirt and wood shavings and was talking to another of the workers. "I don't know."

"You don't know where your daughter's father is?"

"He's gone. Gone!" She threw the words at him. "It doesn't matter, all right! I walked out on him—ran out—and he left, all right! End of story."

"No, not end of story. He has no contact with Susanna?"

"No."

"What about child support? Does he at least provide that?"

"Joe—"

"Is he supporting his daughter?"

"No." Her eyes had widened again until he wondered if her soul would soon be exposed. "He's not."

"You have a right and he has an obligation."

"I don't care. I just want him out of our lives, to feel free and safe." Gasping, she clamped her fingers over her mouth.

He nearly gave her the space she needed but something kept him going. "You aren't doing any of you a favor by shouldering the burden all by yourself. I pay child support; I'd do it even if it wasn't ordered. It makes me feel more like a father."

The words he didn't know he'd been going to say slammed into him, the truth. "Your ex-husband is getting away scot-free and you work for an agency that tries to get parents to accept their responsibilities. I don't get it."

"I'm not asking you to."

"How does Susanna feel about everything?"

"Don't."

He didn't want this, didn't have room for her in his too-full life, but she'd reached him just the same. "You've walked smack into the middle of my life but you're telling me I have no right to know anything about you as a human being? I don't buy it."

She wrapped her arms around her middle again, the gesture pulling her blouse tight over her breasts—breasts that were fuller than he'd realized before and, he guessed, hadn't felt a man's hands on them for a long time. "I don't want this conversation," she said. "You have no right—"

"And you have every right to probe into all aspects of my life?"

She started to shake her head. "There are many things I don't know about you."

"Like what?"

"Like—like other people in your life."

"A woman you mean? Is that what you're asking?"

Before she could confirm or deny that, he plunged on. "There isn't."

"There's no . . ." She took a long, deep breath but didn't say anything.

Once again Joe heard his name being called, and he told Kristen that he had to tend to business. Then, although he knew better, he told her that he'd been thinking about her daughter's conflicting emotions where horses were concerned. "A rodeo might help her understand that, despite their size, they're non-combative animals and even if a man or woman gets thrown, they aren't going to be hurt," he explained.

"You can't promise that."

No, he couldn't. "She'll be in the stands and you'll be with her. She'll sense the excitement, see the clowns, everything. I think she'd enjoy it."

"A rodeo is violent."

"It's physical but it's not violent. At least it isn't if the people running it know what they're doing. Look, there's one coming up next weekend that I'm participating in. Bring her." He rocked forward, shocked by his need to feel her soft and small body against his.

Traffic was horrible and required her full attention. Just the same, the tape continued to play inside Kristen's head. Although she needed to understand how Joe had managed to direct the conversation to what was going on in her life when it should have remained on his situation, she was too busy battling the truth for that. The electrical impulses that had burst to life when she'd been around him earlier had returned today. There hadn't been a moment when she hadn't been aware of him; it had taken all her strength to keep her hands off him.

An older pickup shot out of a side street, forcing her to slam on her brakes. Shaken, she nearly honked her horn, but she'd had all the confrontation she could take for one day.

Joe had gone back to work after issuing his challenge or whatever it was. She should have left; instead, she'd stood leaning against her car's hot door as his powerful legs took him first to Brent's side and then toward the man who'd been calling for him. He wasn't the biggest man at the construction site, but Joe had a presence about him that wordlessly proclaimed him as the one in charge. That's what she'd been watching, his command of his world.

A left turn light switched to red before she could get through. Frustrated, she slammed her hand against the steering wheel. Pain numbed her arm, forcing her out of whatever place she'd been in since leaving Joe. She wasn't a physical woman. She'd never so much as swatted her daughter's behind, but it felt good to hit the steering wheel.

Smiling despite herself, she imagined herself gunning the engine and forcing other drivers to slam on their brakes so she could have her way. She'd grab a sports car, fill it with gas, and head for the open country. With the windows down and music blaring on the radio, she'd sing and yell and—

The image of her foot punching the gas pedal brought her back to reality in time to join the herd of cars slipping under the left turn light. Reckless speed and yelling wasn't for her. Other people might abandon their good sense, and risk life and limb, but she'd never been one of those. She was responsible, conservative. Living a safe, boring life.

No, not boring or safe. Not any more.

Meeting a man with deep, dark eyes and a commanding body had changed things.

SEVEN

A roar of sound greeted Kristen and Susanna as they got out of the car at the rodeo grounds a couple of miles beyond the city limits. Kristen inhaled exhaust fumes and animal scents and an energy which quickly, powerfully seeped into her being. So this too was Joe's world. Her little daughter hung back, taking it all in. "How come everything is so noisy?" Susanna asked, her hands clasped over her ears.

"Maybe because horses and cows have never been in school and don't know how to act," she offered, grinning.

After ruffling Susanna's hair, she took her hand and followed the groups of people heading toward what she took to be the ticket booth. What she could see of the wooden fencing enclosing the arena looked weathered, yet sturdy. She'd driven by numerous times but had never explored further. Tonight, filled with excitement and anticipation while questioning her sanity, she was torn between paying for their seats and running back to what was safe and ordinary.

Joe didn't know she was coming. Although they'd talked several times, their conversations had been about Brent. She'd also approached him about hiring a mentally challenged young man in the process of leaving his parents and moving into a group home. Joe had been willing to consider it but first needed to assure himself that the young man understood safety precautions. She'd agreed to bring Andy to the construction site in a few days.

"What if Joe gets bunked off?" Susanna asked after she'd bought their tickets. "I don't want him to get hurt."

"Neither does he. I'm sure he'll be as careful as he can." If Joe was injured, Susanna would be upset, but all her daughter had talked about for days was seeing what she was certain were 'hundreds and hundreds' of horses, and she'd wanted to give Susanna that opportunity.

Only that wasn't the only reason she'd come.

When she saw the wooden planks they'd be expected to sit on, she was sorry she hadn't brought cushions and glad she'd chosen jeans for both of them. An elderly couple wearing cowboy hats were on her right, but so far there wasn't anyone next to Susanna. The couple smiled at the eager little girl, then launched into an explanation of how their son helped supply the roping stock.

"Is this your first time here?" the woman asked. "I don't recall seeing you before."

Susanna nodded but didn't say anything, prompting Kristen to explain that a friend had invited them but since he was competing, they hadn't come with him.

"Who's your friend? I bet we know him."

"Joe Red Shadow." The name seemed to linger on her lips, and she studied the arena for a glimpse of him.

"He's a cowboy," Susanna offered shyly. "I don't want him to get bunked off."

"Bucked," Kristen corrected with a smile.

"Oh, he won't. He's no longer in the bronc or bull events," the man explained. "Didn't you know that?"

"I-I guess it didn't come up," Kristen offered. "I just assumed—what does he do?"

"Calf roping, and he's one of the best out there. All these young Indians think they can show up the old man, but they have a long way to go."

"Joe isn't old," she said.

"He is for this. Most people's bodies can't take the punishment once the years start piling on. But Joe—" The man shrugged. "He was wild and reckless when he started, didn't seem to care what happened to him. He must have had some powerful luck riding with him because by all rights, he should be gimping around, but he isn't."

Wild. Not willing to let her mind fasten on that word, she turned the conversation to something the man had said. "You mentioned Indians. A lot of them participate in the rodeo, do they?"

Obviously she'd said something that screamed ignorance because the couple stared at her. "This is an all-Indian event," the woman explained. "Something to do with their heritage."

Although she felt the need to justify her unfamiliarity with the situation, her attention was drawn to what was taking place in the large, enclosed oval below. To the left were five numbered stalls, and it was there that most of the activity was taking place. Other men and a few women were riding about, sometimes stopping to talk to other riders or people in the stands, sometimes taking off in a mad and seemingly aimless gallop. The thought of trying to control one of those head-flinging, heavily muscled horses chilled her, but that wasn't all she felt.

The night fairly vibrated with anticipation and excitement, the taste and feel and promise of danger. She swelled with it, became something she'd never been before. Breathing took more and more effort and when the elderly woman handed her her binoculars, she fixed them on the stalls as she sought something she didn't understand but desperately needed.

Lean legs, broad shoulders, muscled forearms. Wild-eyed and snorting broncs, massive bulls threatening to tear apart the enclosures they were being herded into. The world within her vision was nothing more or less than physical, man against animal. Rough and basic. On her way here, she'd struggled with her very real concern that a human or animal might be injured and how she and Susanna would deal with that, but now that didn't matter.

Life was filled with risks. Marrying Susanna's father had been the greatest she'd faced so far. Escaping and then divorcing him had called for just as much courage. Her ancestors and the ancestors of every one of these Indians had lived dangerous and precarious lives; maybe the riders and ropers still carried what of their forebearers' genes had made it possible for them to survive. People like Joe Red Shadow needed, wanted to pit themselves against the odds just as she'd wanted to race a sports car through the night.

When Susanna tugged on her sleeve, she reluctantly freed herself from a little of the rodeo's energy. Her daughter could smell hot dogs.

"Don't worry about someone taking your seats," the woman said. "People are pretty considerate. Besides, if you want to see Joe, you have time to look for him behind the stalls.''

Joe again. But maybe everything tonight was about him. ''I don't want to get in the way.''

''You won't. Things are pretty casual here. Besides.'' The woman winked. ''I'm betting Joe will want to know you're here.''

She would have to do that but had halfway convinced herself that that could wait until after Joe's event. Besides, she needed to see him in the environment he loved, wanted to try to understand more about him, wanted things she couldn't bring herself to articulate or even acknowledge. After getting Susanna a ketchup-laden hot dog and a soft drink, she ran interference as they made their way to where the rodeo's real work was taking place. She noticed a few people who didn't look like contestants milling about, mostly women whose eyes followed their men's movements.

Insanely, she wanted to be one of those women. In her fantasy, Joe's face would light up when he saw her and he'd lean down from his saddle while she stretched toward him and their lips would meet. Her eyes would speak of pride and concern and a promise of what the rest of the night could be for them. His own eyes would carry the same message—when he was done doing this thing he was so good at, they would find a time and place to be alone. There wouldn't be any need for words. Action, a quick disrobing followed by hungry exploration would culminate in—

''Mommy?''

''What?'' She sounded stupid and out of breath and was very glad her five year old daughter didn't yet know about a woman's yearnings.

"They all look the same. We'll never be able to find him."

"Maybe you're right."

"Mommy?"

"What?"

"How come all those big cows are here?" She pointed at the corral holding bulls with massive heads and bodies that reminded her of earthmoving equipment. The creatures looked strangely docile when what little she knew about them led her to believe they spent their lives bent on destroying anything and everything they could.

"They're not cows, Susanna," a deep voice said. Kristen looked up.

Joe. How he'd managed to spot them in this mess of humanity was beyond her, but she wouldn't ask. He wore expensive cowboy boots, jeans that looked as if they'd been created for his body alone, a longsleeved, pearl button shirt open at the throat to reveal the feather resting against his throat. His hat was ringed with what she suspected was rattlesnake skin. She couldn't see enough of his eyes, a fact which made her wonder how much her own revealed.

She'd been hit by his impact just as she'd known she'd be; she should have marshaled her defenses. Fighting the lingering memory of the wanton thoughts that had swept over her while she was looking for him, Kristen struggled to find something to talk about, but he spoke first.

"I didn't think you'd come," he said.

"I didn't either.

"Why did you?"

What an impossibly hard question. It had a great deal to do with knowing they could work together for

Brent's good. Susanna's ongoing fascination with him also factored in, but it was more, much more. Private and primitive. Kristen pointed discreetly at her daughter, who was taking in Joe's attire, specifically the leather belt with its silver buckle decorated with a carved eagle's head, which only served to highlight his lean waist.

"Life can get boring even for a five year old," Kristen said. "I decided she needed a new experience."

He looked at her, tantalizing her with the question of what he was thinking about. She loved his rich, thick hair and wished he hadn't covered it. Still, the hat made him even more a part of his surroundings and defined him as a cowboy. An Indian cowboy wearing a black hat.

"I could have gotten you tickets if you'd told me," he said.

"I—I wasn't sure about coming back here, but the couple I was talking to said it was all right," she told him. "I hope we're not in the way."

"You aren't, and I'm glad you came."

Are you? If you know that, maybe you can tell me how I should be feeling. "I'm sorry. You must have things you should be doing."

"Not yet. The riding events come first."

Which meant he had time for her—them, but knowing that only made things more complicated. Darn it, she didn't belong here. His world intimidated and fascinated her almost as much as the man himself did. How much easier this would be if he'd come to her office and they had professional, official things to talk about.

"Joe?"

"What, young lady?"

Immensely relieved now that Joe was no longer holding onto her with his eyes, she concentrated on the conversation between man and girl. Susanna, her attention darting here and there, wanted to know what to call the big, dirty creatures if they weren't cows.

"Brahma bulls," Joe explained. "They all have those humps on their backs."

"Why?"

He laughed, the sound rich and full and honest. "That's a good question. Maybe so they can look mean. What do you think? Could you ride one of them?"

Susanna's eyes widened. "No way! They're too gigantic!"

"That's no reason to be afraid of them," a youthful male voice said.

Sensing his presence, Kristen acknowledged Brent. The boy was dressed essentially the same as his uncle and looked innately Apache. Joe had said he'd been hopeful he was making headway in convincing Brent that understanding his heritage was important; maybe this was proof. Obviously aware that he had an attentive audience in little Susanna, Brent explained that Brahmas hated having anyone on their backs and all but turned themselves inside out attempting to rid themselves of the unwanted burden, but left alone, they were mild-mannered animals.

"You can even feed them if you want to," he informed Susanna.

"No way!" Susanna insisted before Kristen was forced into protective mother mode. "They might eat my hand."

Brent snorted. Just the same, he didn't seem to be in a hurry to dismiss her. Instead, he told her how much his boots had cost and that he'd started riding his uncle's horses and as soon as he'd had a little more practice, he intended to compete. Susanna continued to stare at him as if he was the most fascinating person she'd ever met.

"What do you think of this place?" Joe asked her. "Do you understand what's going on?"

Susanna started to nod, then shook it. "I didn't know horses were that big."

"They are, aren't they, but you'll get better at drawing them if you're around them."

That obviously made sense to Susanna who, to Kristen's surprise, accepted Joe's offer to pet his horse. She nearly objected when the sleek, nervous-looking animal pawed the ground, but in the end she didn't because Joe had taken her daughter's hand and she couldn't take her eyes off the way his swallowed the smaller one. Joe would never let anything happen to Susanna.

She hung back, hoping to watch the interplay between the two from a distance but was distracted when she realized Brent still stood beside her.

"What do you think of what your uncle does?" she asked. "You really think you want to try competing?"

"Yeah, I do. Mom and I used to watch him, so I know how good he is."

A little hero worship wasn't bad, she thought, wondering if Susanna would come away from the evening's events feeling the same way. She probably should ask Brent how he was doing at school but it was Friday night and when she'd been that age, the last thing she'd wanted to talk about on a weekend was school. Still, she was a social worker and Brent was her responsibility.

"How's it going between the two of you?" she asked. "Joe helping you with your homework?"

"Some. Most of it I can do on my own."

"I'm glad to hear that," she said, then asked about his and his uncle's evening ritual. Joe had set up a schedule which made it possible for Brent to spend his afternoons working but once dinner was over, the TV went off and Brent did his homework while Joe tended to construction business paperwork.

"It sounds as if the two of you are pretty organized."

"Yeah, well, I guess."

Wondering if there was a universal language of kids designed to let adults know something was wrong, she prompted him to be more specific.

"It's all that nonsense with legends and stories," the boy grumbled. "The one he's working on now supposedly tells how Apaches learned to cure sick people with chants and ceremonies. He can't be serious! I mean, no one's going to believe there was this—whatever he was—called the One Who Made the Earth who got some old men to heal a couple of sick warriors because he taught them songs about lightning and stuff. Get real!"

"I don't think the stories are to be taken literally."

"Big deal. They're stupid."

She could have gone into a complex conversation about religion and belief systems but suspected that would turn Brent off. "This really bothers you, doesn't it?" she asked.

"Yeah. It's like he becomes someone else when he's working on those things. He gets this spaced-out look and he tries to find deep meaning in stuff when it's not there."

Deep meaning. Yes, Joe would do that. "A lot of people

want to understand where they came from and what life was like for their ancestors."

"Fine. Only I'm not interested. Like, you know, that feather he wears. It's supposed to be sacred 'cause only Indians can have eagle feathers. He wants me to wear one, but I won't."

She wasn't going to ask Brent to explain his resistance, but both Joe and Brent were going to have to bend a little if things were going to work out between them. Seeking distraction, she started toward Joe and Susanna who were still standing beside Joe's mare. She stopped after taking three or four steps, her attention fixed on what was happening. Joe was holding the horse's reins but his grip was pretty casual, considering how big the animal was. Susanna was fascinated, but at the same time, her body language spoke of hesitancy and a little fear. She'd inched toward Joe until she stood with her shoulder against his side. Although he wasn't looking at Susanna, there was no doubt that Joe was aware of a great deal about her.

He was, she realized, acting like a father.

"What do you think?" she asked her daughter when she trusted herself to speak. "Their hair is pretty soft, isn't it?"

Susanna reached out to touch the mare's irresistibly velvety nose. She jumped when the horse breathed out, but Joe muttered something and she kept her hand where it was. She even giggled when the animal nuzzled her palm. From where she stood, Kristen drew comparisons between her daughter's five year old body and an animal capable of running down half grown steers. Susanna trusted someone, Joe, enough to let a fifteen hundred pound animal touch her.

Joe. Although she warned herself not to do it, she

again studied him. She doubted that he'd ever stepped inside a fitness gym, but his physique would put many body builders to shame because he was designed for honest labor. His face bore the impact of the elements. He'd told her about broken bones and scars; his body wasn't perfect. It didn't matter.

Someone yelled at Joe. With his attention still on Susanna and his mare, he answered. From what Kristen understood, one of the arena helpers hadn't shown up and Joe was needed to help the bronc riders dismount after a ride, if they weren't thrown.

"Sorry," he told Susanna. "Duty calls. How about if you and your mom keep an eye on me so you can tell me how I'm doing?"

Susanna said something Kristen didn't catch because just then one of the Brahmas bellowed. Not bothering to try to be heard herself, she gestured to indicate that Susanna was to join her. Susanna hadn't reached her by the time Joe swung into the saddle.

He rode his head-tossing horse as if he'd never done anything else in life and was willing to die doing exactly this. Feeling suddenly deprived of oxygen, she worked at expanding her lungs but couldn't think about anything except him, his message, his image.

Joe Red Shadow was a man for a muscled, physical world and feared nothing that world might throw at him. He understood and accepted it. Loved it. He probably expected any woman he loved or who loved him to embrace his universe wholeheartedly. Kristen wondered if she'd ever be up to that challenge.

EIGHT

Somehow, Kristen had managed to get her daughter and herself back to their seats. She'd watched Joe enter the arena but then had lost sight of him and felt out of place around all those cowboys, horses, and bulls. Besides, Susanna had started hugging her side again. The elderly couple they'd been sitting beside had welcomed them with questions about whether she'd found Joe. When they asked Susanna what she thought of Joe's horse, the little girl replied enthusiastically.

"What is it with girls and horses?" the woman asked. "I've always loved them. They intimidated me all right, but I had a collection of at least a hundred plastic horse figures and would play with them by the hour. What about you, young lady? I bet you have posters of them."

"Not yet, but I'm going to soon. And I draw them all the time."

Brent joined them about then. He seemed intrigued by Susanna, and Kristen couldn't help but wonder if it hadn't occurred to him that she might have a life beyond being a social worker. Instead of reminding herself of how important the separation between her professional and private life had always been to her, she'd walked, eyes open, into Joe Red Shadow's world.

The reality of that became increasingly clear as the rodeo progressed. Whenever she saw him, Joe was all movement and energy. Seemingly filled with a sense about where he would be needed, he continually surfaced in the middle of whatever action suddenly exploded. If a bronc rider was thrown and the horse took off in a mad dash, Joe was right behind him. Sometimes he used his unbelievably accurate rope throws to bring the animal to a halt, but most times he simply made sure his mount hugged the other creature's side and didn't hurt itself.

Those around her talked constantly and she was aware of holding up her end of casual conversations, especially Susanna's need for explanation of what was happening, but Joe's impact never left her. One of the things she loved about living in New Mexico was being able to go out into the country where she could watch hawks and other birds of prey as they prowled the sky. Joe was like that, a commanding presence completely in control, at home.

Heat surged through her and although she tried to pull free by concentrating on Brent's explanation to Susanna that the clowns' true role wasn't to entertain the crowd but to protect thrown riders from being hurt by the Brahma bulls, she continued to feel alive and aware in a way she didn't understand—or maybe understood all too well.

She'd married Susanna's father because she thought she was in love, because she'd wanted to feel as if she belonged to someone. Sex had been all right at first, a little disappointing because it took Cliff such a short time to satisfy himself, but she'd come to him as a virgin and had nothing to compare with. And then his temper—

But her marriage was behind her. All except for the memories and hard lessons learned. The future stretched ahead, and for the first time since she'd walked out on her ex, she'd started to question whether she wanted to spend the rest of her life alone.

What would Joe look like waiting for—for his bride—to walk down the aisle? Kristen tried to imagine him in a tux, his hair slicked back and his feet in something besides boots. If he loved the woman enough, he'd try to mold himself into the required image, but he'd still wear his eagle feather under his starched shirt, and the hand sporting a brand new wedding ring would be rough and work-ready.

He'd smile at his bride, lift her veil and cover her willing mouth with his own. When the wedding and reception and well-wishing was over, he'd lift that woman in his strong arms and carry her into his bedroom. A full moon would drape its silver light over them as they—

"Mommy?"

"Y-es, honey."

"When I'm bigger, can I have a horse?"

Unprepared for the question and the abrupt end to her fantasy, she could only stare at her daughter. Then she gathered her arguments, but before she could speak, she caught Brent's eye and discovered amusement lighting up his face. She wouldn't be surprised if he'd put Susanna up to her request. Thankfully neither of them had any inkling where her mind had been when they'd cooked up their little plot.

"I'll tell you what," she said, working at keeping her voice even. "If Brent will promise to come over every day and take care of it, especially the cleaning up part, we'll see."

"Will you?" Susanna demanded of Brent. "I'm not tall enough to put on a saddle. You'll have to do it and teach me how to ride."

"Sure, no sweat," Brent replied. She thought he might elaborate, but at that moment, a blaring loud-speaker made conversation all but impossible. When Brent clapped, she concentrated on what was being said. The roping events were about to begin.

Accompanied by her own private thoughts, she scanned the arena. Not being able to study Joe should have made dismissing his impact easier, but the thought was still forming when she admitted she was lying to herself. The anticipation of waiting for him to appear built and grew until she felt consumed. She shouldn't let go of her self-control this way, shouldn't allow her fantasies to run free! She was a responsible member of the middle class, a tax paying, newspaper reading, voting woman with a child to support, not a fantasizing, wanton—

Roper after roper exploded into the arena. She lost herself in speed and noise, clapping wildly not just because she appreciated a skilled cowboy and well-trained horse but because she couldn't sit still. If she did, whatever was threatening to consume her would surely succeed.

Finally it was Joe's turn. He rode his mare as if they came from the same body. With one hand oh-so-lightly on the reins, he used the other to snake his rope surely and swiftly over the pounding steer's head. When the rope settled into place, his mare stopped so suddenly that her haunches brushed the ground. Before the steer could regain its balance, Joe catapulted himself out of the saddle, grabbed its horns and flipped it onto its side. His hands were a blur of practiced movement as he secured three legs, then he stepped back and threw his hands into the air signaling a successful tie. A moment later his time was announced and applause erupted.

"Just anyone try to beat that!" Brent exclaimed. "The old man's still got it."

"He's hardly an old man," Kristen insisted, still clapping wildly.

"Yeah, but I have to give him a hard time about it," he yelled back.

Joe had untied the steer and was helping it to its feet when, with an indignant bellow, it ran off. Joe looked as if he'd spent his entire life standing in the dust in the middle of a rodeo arena with hundreds of people sharing in his victory. Fire danced through her, danced and caught and flamed, and she didn't try to tell herself she didn't know its cause.

At this moment the only thing she wanted out of life was to make love to Joe Red Shadow. His hard and competent body would mold itself to hers. She'd cling to him, lose herself in him, freely and joyfully allow her essence to melt into his.

But it couldn't be.

Joe's shoulder burned and he'd be fighting stiffness in the morning, but he knew how to treat the bumps and bruises that were part of rodeoing. After loosening his mare's cinch, he wiped his sweaty hands on his jeans. No matter how many times he'd performed in this event, he'd never been able to eliminate the nervousness that came while waiting his turn, but tension

helped him concentrate on what he was determined
to do and thus lessened the possibility of injury.

But he was done competing for the night; other
thoughts were free to enter—one thought, the question of what Kristen had seen and how she'd reacted.

This place wasn't her domain. She was all softness
and quiet, a gentle woman who surrounded herself
with peace. A small part of him argued that someone
who worked at the job she had and was raising a child
by herself was far from sheltered, but tonight he
wanted to place her in the dream world he'd created.
He would give her roses and wildflowers and she'd
show her appreciation with a sweet smile and a sweet
kiss.

No, he didn't want to think of her like that after all.
Tonight with his muscles still hot from the effort of
wrestling a four hundred pound steer to the ground,
he needed a woman with fire in her veins and hunger
in her belly.

Kristen would know what he wanted, and there'd
be no dancing around the issue of their becoming
lovers. Both innocent and experienced, she'd stand
naked before him. His own clothes would fall to the
floor, and because there'd only be moonlight, they'd
appear like silver shadows to each other. Neither
would speak because their bodies would be saying everything. Who and what they were to each other once
the day began didn't matter because at night with the
desert-scented breeze coming in the window, they'd
simply be a man and a woman. Their lovemaking—

"Not bad for an old man."

Both resenting and grateful for the distraction, he
glared at his nephew. Susanna, looking both thrilled

and scared, stood beside him, and Kristen waited behind them.

"What did you think?" He asked the question of the girl, but his attention was on the woman.

Susanna muttered something he took to be awe. He had no idea what Kristen's reaction had been or maybe the truth was that his fantasy about her still held him.

"I'm going to teach Susanna how to ride a horse," Brent announced. "Once she knows how, her mom's going to buy her one."

"Wait a minute," Kristen interjected. "I said we'd see."

"We'll see." Brent gave Susanna a gentle punch on the arm. "That's what grown-ups say when they don't want to have to think about something."

Before he could prepare himself, Kristen's ready laughter bubbled up. "You think you've got me pegged, don't you, Brent?" she asked.

"I'm right, aren't I?"

"Yes," she conceded. "You are. However, we live in an apartment. There's no way the landlord's going to let us keep one."

Joe hadn't allowed himself to give much thought to where Kristen lived, but now he wanted to walk through her rooms until he understood what she'd done to make it hers. He imagined her being a whole made up of two very different halves. There was the competent professional who existed forty hours a week, but he knew he wasn't wrong in his assessment of her feminine and gentle side—something that had never been part of his world.

"An apartment?" he asked. "Do you like it?"

"No, but it's going to have to do until I've saved enough for a down payment on a house."

"Hm. Do you have one in mind?"

"That would only make me more discontent, but I've been known to spend a Sunday afternoon going to open houses."

"What appeals to you?"

She answered immediately. "An older place, maybe not quite as isolated as yours, but I want a decent size yard so I can grow flowers. I've looked at enough new homes to know they don't have enough character for me—at least the ones I can afford don't. Besides, I like the idea of doing some fixing up."

With every word she spoke, she came more alive. Obviously, having her own home meant a great deal to her, and despite her contention that it was counterproductive to fantasize about what she couldn't yet have, she'd done a great deal of it. Yes, he could see her down on hands and knees while she planted new flowers and bushes. She'd spend hours looking for just the right curtains and color of paint and take pleasure from every one of those hours. Like the hummingbird of one of the legends, she was a nester. A nester without a mate.

Because it was safer not to allow her to make any more of an inroad on his senses, Joe turned his attention to the children. In them he saw the same dichotomy that existed between him and Kristen. Susanna, despite her practical apparel, was a sweet child with her soft blond hair held away from her face by a bright yellow ribbon while Brent, like him, was all dark blues and brown. Was that it? He was earth and rock while Kristen danced with rainbows?

Without asking if he wanted him to do it, Brent took

his horse's reins and told him he'd cool her down and get her settled in her stall. Surprised by the generous offer, he asked what Brent wanted in return.

The boy grinned. "A little gratuity wouldn't hurt. And if you wanted to drop me off at the matinee tomorrow, that wouldn't bother me either."

"I'm taking you to see your grandfather tomorrow, not that I think you've forgotten."

"Why can't he come here?"

"Because he hates leaving the reservation; you know that."

"And I hate going out there."

"Brent, this isn't the place or time to discuss that."

"Then when? Your forcing me to do something isn't going to change the way I feel."

No, it wasn't, but he'd meant what he'd said when he told Brent that this wasn't the time or place to bring up their disagreement. Not only didn't he want to drag Kristen into this, but Susanna was watching them with slowly widening eyes, and her little body had begun to tremble.

"Susanna, how would you like to go with Brent?" he offered. "He might even let you take the reins."

"Joe, no."

"It's all right," he reassured Kristen who'd taken a protective step toward her daughter. "Brent won't let anything happen to her." Watching the boy out of the corner of his eye, he observed a lessening in his tension. Still, they had a long way to go before they'd resolve the issue which had prompted their argument.

"*I* won't let anything happen to her," Kristen said. Her tone was sharp.

"It won't. I promise."

"You can't—"

"Mommy, it's all right. I'm not afraid."

Kristen looked down at her daughter with an expression that went straight to his heart. Resignation more than agreement tinged her words as she gave approval for the two children to go off together as long as Susanna was back in ten minutes.

"Kristen," Joe began once they were alone. "I wouldn't have suggested it if I had any question about her safety. Babe has nerves of steel and is unbelievably easy to handle."

"But she kept pawing and snorting earlier."

"Because she loves roping. Babe is the first horse my own daughter rode."

"I—I'm glad to hear that." Kristen took a deep and telling breath. "I just hope she gets over her fascination with horses before—"

"What are you afraid of?"

He readied himself for her denial. Instead, she ran her hand through her hair, the gesture telling him a little about how hard it was for her to expose certain things about herself to him.

Sighing, she began. "Something happened a long time ago . . . Joe? Have you ever seen your daughter in danger?"

"No."

"It's different for me."

"How?"

"How?" she repeated and he was certain that was going to be the end of it. Then: "I—I think I want to tell you about it."

She started to slide her hands into her pockets but wound up hugging her middle instead which made him think of a lost child. "It was—she was only three."

Three. Still a baby.

"I couldn't let him!" She pounded out the words. "I would have done anything to stop him, even killed him if that's what it had taken. Nothing mattered except protecting her."

"Him?"

"Susanna's father."

Fighting rage, he pulled Kristen against him. It wasn't until he felt her warmth that he realized what he'd done, but it was too late, and he didn't care. "What happened?"

"It was his temper; it was always his temper."

"Did he hurt her? What about you?"

Kristen pulled back enough that she could look at him, but she hadn't indicated she wanted him to release her. Until she did, he would give her what sense of security he could and fight to contain the male in him. "I shouldn't be doing this," she whispered. "Our relationship—"

"Kristen, we're two human beings tonight, nothing more. What brought us together in the first place doesn't matter."

"Do you really believe that?"

He couldn't say what he believed, just that she needed to be free of certain things and he wanted to help make that happen for her. "Start by answering me this. Did he hurt her?"

"No. But he would have if I hadn't stopped him."

"What did you do?"

"Do? Cliff's temper—he couldn't control it."

"Was Susanna afraid of him?"

Although a shudder wracked her body, she didn't cry. "Joe, it started so slowly, so insidiously that I didn't know . . . That's not right. I knew something horrible was taking place, but I never expected. . . ." She stopped to compose herself. "When I married him, I had no idea what he was capable of. I kept telling myself he was under a lot of stress trying to support a family, but my father did the same thing and he's the gentlest man I've ever known."

"Did you tell your parents what was happening?"

"No." A couple of mounted cowboys passed by so closely that a flipping tail brushed Kristen's shoulder but she didn't seem to notice. "I didn't know how. I was so proud of myself for having gotten through college and marrying, as if it had made me an honest to goodness adult. I'm not very big. Dad always called me his little princess; I loved it."

He could almost hear the pride and protection in her father's voice as he had said that.

"That's the way it was with Cliff at first." Kristen was no longer looking up at him. Instead she seemed fascinated by something at her feet.

Her voice small and yet strong, she told him about walking down the aisle next to a man who'd been a military policeman and had just been hired by the county correctional system. She'd applied for every job she could but because of her lack of experience, she'd wound up doing work for a temporary agency. Cliff didn't mind because he liked having her waiting for him. As long as their conversation revolved around what mattered to him, they never argued.

"His job was part of the problem," she told him. "He was a prison guard. He used to say he had to put on his mean face there so the inmates wouldn't take advantage of him. I think that somewhere along the line it stopped being playacting."

The rodeo was winding down. Joe had been in first place following his ride but didn't know whether anyone else had come in with a better score. He would find out later.

"The job didn't do it to him, Kristen," he said. "His personality had been formed long before that."

"That's what my parents said when I finally told them I'd left Cliff. My father is such a quiet, mild-mannered man, but he wanted to kill Cliff."

He couldn't remember when he'd taken his hand off her. He did know he hadn't wanted to, but she'd started moving about restlessly and holding onto her had become impossible. Still she remained close enough that he hoped she could draw some strength from him. "What happened?"

"I—I couldn't remember when he wasn't angry. I'd spend my days watching the clock and dreading when he'd come in the door. He wasn't physically abusive; I wouldn't have stayed if he'd been. But I felt surrounded by his temper. It was everything. He broke furniture, put his fist through a wall twice. His driving—it got to where I refused to get in the car with him because he was so aggressive."

He needed to know why she hadn't left the first time Cliff buried his fist in a wall but maybe she didn't have an answer.

"Then one night I told him he either had to get help controlling his temper or I was leaving him. That was the end."

"Good."

She shook her head. "My honesty nearly killed us."

By 'us' she meant Susanna as well. *Tell me,* Joe said with his eyes, his fingers now brushing the side of her throat while he assured himself that she'd come out of that night in one piece.

"He, ah, he went crazy. Told me he was in charge and I would do what he said. Then he hit me."

Feeling a little crazy himself, he forced himself to remain silent.

"Then he grabbed Susanna, lifted her over his head."

No!

"He was going to throw her. I knew—"

Kristen's hands were caught in his now; he felt so much in their heat and trembling.

"I screamed and screamed but he didn't look at me."

Don't stop now. Keep it coming; we'll deal with the consequences later.

"Susanna's face turned red. I thought she was going to cry or beg him to stop but she just stared at me. She was such a little thing, a trusting child in the grip of a monster."

Keep it coming.

"I hit him."

"Good."

"I remember—I felt as if I was falling apart inside. There was this big, angry man and he had my child in his arms and I knew that I'd die before I let him hurt her."

A couple of cowboys started his way but he silently warned them off.

"I punched him in the stomach, hit him with everything in me. That's when he finally looked at me, but he didn't let go of her and I knew I was capable of killing him."

"Mother bear protecting her young."

"Mother grizzly." She laughed, the sound not a whimper but hard and knowing. "I told him I'd kill him if he didn't put her down. He—I think he must have been trying to show me he could do whatever he wanted and there wasn't anything I could do to stop him. He was wrong."

Keep it coming.

"That's when I kicked him," she said with another of those laughless laughs. "Only this time I didn't aim for his stomach."

Imagining a shoe where it would do the most good, he nodded approval.

"He started to drop her. That's when I grabbed her."

Although her description was sketchy, he imagined mother and daughter landing in a heap as Kristen fought to cushion her daughter's fall. He wouldn't allow himself to form an image of what would have happened if Cliff Childers had followed through on his insane impulse to smash his daughter against the hard surface.

"You were both all right?" He brought her hands to his mouth and covered her palms with kisses.

"We left that night," she whispered. She was staring at their joined fingers. "I never went back to him."

And you've been alone ever since. Joe understood the wariness in her eyes at last.

NINE

Joe had kissed her. His unexpected tenderness awakened the nerves in her palms and took her into a place where sensation and reaction ruled. In a dim way she knew she should be asking herself what she'd told him and why she'd revealed too much, but it was a warm New Mexico evening and the crowds had thinned out, leaving them in their own separate space.

"You're no hothouse flower," he said with his breath puffing against the inside of her wrists.

"A hot—? No."

"That's the way I thought of you when I first saw you, and here, too, because you're small and feminine. But what you did that night was something Daddy's little princess never could."

Although the experience had been more desperate self-preservation and mother instinct than anything else, she looked back on the actions she'd taken with pride. "Nothing matters more than Susanna's safety and happiness," she told him. The simple statement said everything.

"Rampaging grizzly?"

This time Kristen could smile. "The veneer of civilization turned out to be pretty thin," she admitted, still not free of this man's effect on her. "You wouldn't have recognized me then."

"Maybe. Maybe not."

He was saying something about what he believed he knew about her, and she wanted to follow the subject along whatever path it took but couldn't dismiss his impact on her senses. Someone had started turning off the lights which had illuminated the arena, and she felt this strange and exciting world begin to quiet. Shadows caught at Joe and made him indistinct, more image than man. Still she remained acutely aware of his substance, his presence, his impact.

Tonight she wanted to feel nothing except his kisses and the quality she'd already sensed, which lay deeper than gentleness and hesitancy.

She didn't want to be a mother right now, but she was.

"I have to find her," she made herself say. "She doesn't like being alone in the dark."

"Brent's with her."

"But she doesn't know him that well. Joe?" Reluctantly she pulled free. "She was traumatized by her father's temper. I didn't know how bad it was until we were away from him and I could think again. She's getting better. At least she's getting better."

"So are you."

"Yes, I am." She should have stepped further away from him, either that or he should have been the one to set a safe distance between them, but it was too late for that, and her mouth longed for what her hand had experienced.

"Kristen?"

"What?"

"You're a beautiful woman."

His words were dangerous, but instead of running away, she allowed herself to look into the danger. Moths congregated around the one remaining light, their presence making Joe's features flicker. Lost to reality, she took a gliding step forward. He did the same, then held out his hands and her own went to them. He was no longer offering her comfort and compassion; they were simply a man and a woman alone together on a summer night.

"We . . . we can't . . ." she tried.

"I know."

"We shouldn't . . ."

"I know."

With their hands trapped between them, what happened wasn't so much an embrace as an awkward reaching for each other's body. Her eyes closed of their own volition and she welcomed the darkness, allowed her other senses to take over. Although it was beginning to cool off, she could still feel the heat of him and knew that hers matched it.

How long had she wanted to kiss him? Maybe from the first moment she'd seen him, but now wasn't the time or place to seek the answer. It pleased her to discover that at least one part of his anatomy was soft. His mouth with its expressive lines opened slightly and she did the same. She wasn't so far gone that she made the mistake of inviting him in but the promise was there.

Promise and danger—and for these precious heart-beats of time, an end to loneliness. It was pure insanity and perhaps the most sane thing she'd ever done. She was coming alive as a woman once more.

"We shouldn't," he whispered, his lips sliding against hers.

"I know," she mouthed. "Joe, I don't want—"

"Neither do I."

Something that might have been a groan escaped him and he rocked away from her. He might have been the one with the presence of mind to put an end to this—whatever it was, but at least she knew to draw her hands free and ram them into her back pockets. Darkness had claimed so much of the grounds that she felt disoriented. Like the moths, her mind flitted here and there, wondering what had happened to the woman she'd always thought she was, finally settling on the only thing it dared. Joe had assured her that Brent knew horses, but what if the boy grew tired of having a little girl trail after him? He might leave her, and she'd feel abandoned and alone in a strange place. Fears that she'd spent the last two years putting behind her rose in a sudden surge, but she fought to keep it to herself.

Careful not to reveal too much in her movements, she peered into the shadows. When a high-pitched giggle reached her, relief poured through her.

"Susanna. Honey. Where are you?" she called.

Brent and her daughter appeared with Babe plodding a step behind them. "Mommy!" Suannna exclaimed. "Can I be a jockey when I grow up?"

"A jockey?" Kristen wanted to look at Joe but didn't dare until her nerves quit humming. Thank goodness the children hadn't seen! "Whatever made you think of that?"

"It's neat. I'm not very heavy," Susanna chattered on. "Horses can carry me and still go really, really fast. I'd win all the races and make lots and lots of money."

Guessing Brent had planted that idea, she nearly asked the boy if he'd explained the realities of such a dangerous career, but her daughter had already proclaimed her determination to become a ballerina, a post man, and a professional finder of lost kittens.

"So you'd like to be a jockey, would you?" Joe asked. "How would you like to ride Babe?"

Susanna's mouth dropped open.

"You don't have to chase a steer or go after a bronc," Joe reassured Susanna. "I just thought you'd like to sit up there and take in the view."

"Joe," Kristen warned. "Don't push her."

"I'm not," he returned. "She can say no if she doesn't want to."

"I don't know," Susanna stalled. "I might fall off."

"You won't," Kristen heard herself say. "Joe won't let you."

At that, Joe turned to her and she saw, or thought she saw, the same disbelief she felt.

Did it really happen? he seemed to be asking.

Yes, she was forced to respond silently. *Yes, it did.*

"Mommy?" Susanna took a deep breath. "Babe isn't a bronc, is she?"

"What? No, she isn't, honey. She's a very well trained horse."

"And she wouldn't hurt me, would she?"

I'll never let anything hurt you again. "No, she won't."

Something in her tone might have made an impact on Joe because he focused, really focused on her, and she remembered not just the essence of their kiss, but what had poured out of her when she'd been unable to keep anything from him. After telling Susanna what she needed to do once she was on Babe, he lifted the little girl and deposited her on the broad back.

"She might wiggle her skin," he explained as he handed Susanna the reins. "She's not used to being ridden without a saddle, or by someone as light as you. Well, what do you think?"

Susanna was concentrating on the thrill and adventure and awe of being on horseback for the first time. As an infant, her face had spoken volumes about what was going on inside her, but over the years, she'd begun to learn the adult art of keeping her emotions to herself. Not tonight, however.

"Well, what do you think?" Kristen echoed Joe's question.

Susanna had one hand wrapped tightly around the reins, and the other gripped the mane. She stared at a spot between Babe's ears, and her short legs stuck out instead of following the lines of Babe's belly. "She's big."

Chuckling, Joe patted Susanna's ankle. "She won't seem so big after you get used to her. Can you feel her breathing?"

"Is that what she's doing?"

"It sure is," Joe reassured. "She worked hard tonight. It'd probably take a cannon going off right next to her to get her to move. In fact, if you sit very still, she just might fall asleep."

He stood so close to Babe that if the mare made a sudden move, his foot might get smashed, but Kristen believed he hadn't stepped back because he knew Susanna would feel more secure with him nearby, him, not her right now.

Instead of resenting his intrusion into what she'd long shared with her daughter, she once more surrendered to fantasy. There couldn't be a more physical world than where they were and now that most of the crowd had cleared out, the essence of the place, of the night made even more of an impact. After what had happened between them, she should know better, but she lacked the will or desire to fight illusion.

Joe was more than flesh and bone. Innately at home here, he'd become part of his surroundings and in his blood flowed the courage of the other Indians who'd competed tonight. He was part of the clean, cooling wind, strong as the stoutest corral, as wild as any bronc.

She believed in his courage, thrilled to his wild nature, needed his strength. Needed him helping her to truly learn what it was to be a woman. But—and this was what returned her to sanity—he couldn't know what she was thinking or needing. Yes, he'd held her and kissed first her palms and then her mouth and given her the reckless strength to share her painful past; shouldn't he want more of that sharing? Instead, his attention was now locked on Susanna and despite the shadows that promised to claim him, she sensed that some of the darkness and distance came from inside him.

Brent had wandered off somewhere, but she couldn't think about him because she was learning yet something more about Joe. It seemed to her that he'd begun to fade into himself. He looked tired, the weariness having nothing to do with what he'd accomplished tonight. It was ludicrous to think she could possibly understand what was going on inside him but maybe their few moments alone together had opened a small pathway between them.

"What is it?" she whispered. "What's going on inside you?"

Joe no longer extended a hand toward Susanna. The strength and substance of him had faded a little, and he looked terribly alone. Although she hurt for him, it went beyond that. When she first fled Cliff, she hadn't been able to talk to anyone about her experience. She might not be able to give Joe comfort, or even understanding, but she could give him his space.

"Susanna," she whispered. "It's getting late. We'd better go."

Susanna piped up and argued that she'd only felt Babe breathe eleven times and didn't want to get down until she'd counted to a hundred, but before Kristen could say anything, Joe placed his hands around the girl's waist and eased her off. Susanna was obviously disappointed, but she didn't say anything and neither did Joe. Instead, he spun away and began leading Babe toward the parking lot where his horse trailer waited.

Whatever time and distance you need, take it. And when you're done, I'll—I'll be waiting, Kristen silently promised.

Babe's shod hooves hitting the packed gravel made a rhythm that matched the pounding of his heart, Joe thought. Kristen's daughter had said she wanted to count his mare's heartbeats. He was sorry she couldn't do that tonight, but her mother was right. It was getting late, and he had to go home.

Liar.

Susanna's laughter was so hard to take. No matter how much he tried to numb his senses to its impact, he failed miserably. He'd missed so much of his daughter's early years that he didn't know when she'd learned how to count; that's what kept bombarding him now, cruel reminders of years lost. If only he'd been older, wiser, less afraid. If he had, he wouldn't have run from what he'd believed was an unwanted responsibility— but he had missed his child's growing up.

Now April was twelve and on the brink of woman-

hood. He'd arranged to have her fly out here as soon
as school was over, and the waiting seemed intermina-
ble, but what would he talk to a budding teenager about
when he didn't know enough about the child she'd
been?

If he remained around Kristen, would he blurt out
his regrets about those precious lost years? She, with
her mother's heart and social worker's wisdom and
woman's instinct, might see into the depths and darkness of him. Would he survive the scrutiny?

Loading Babe into the horse trailer gave him a few
moments' distraction from his swirling thoughts, but
he'd opened the truck's cab door before what he was
doing fully registered. He had to go back for Brent,
but that meant he might have to face Kristen again.

"What is it, Joe?" a soft female voice whispered.

He jumped at the unexpected question but then he
shouldn't have been surprised that Kristen had followed him.

"What is it?" she repeated.

Reluctant, he followed the sound of her voice until
he was looking at her shadowy form not far enough
away. She shouldn't be that hard to dismiss, but he'd
be lying if he tried to convince himself of that. Making
the decision to kiss her hadn't been a decision after
all. It had happened because there was no other way
their time alone together could be played out.

"Like you said, it's late."

"I know. Joe, if you don't want to talk, I understand.
But I trusted you enough to tell you about my past. I
hope you feel the same way. Something's eating you
up and if there's anything I can do . . ."

She'd seen that? "We're doing something dangerous. Something unwise," he said, trying to sound wise when he felt like a fool.

"I know."

"Do you really? I can't for a moment forget that whether I get to keep Brent depends to a great extent on you."

"Yes, it does."

Beyond the rodeo grounds was a vast stretch of undeveloped land which served as home for thousands of night creatures. The melody of crickets began before she spoke again. "You invited me out here," she said. "Maybe I shouldn't have come, but I did. I wound up telling you much more than I ever thought I would. It's too late to pretend that didn't happen."

Did she regret what had poured out of her? Joe wanted her to know he was glad she trusted him enough to reveal so much and he hoped it had helped. But if she thought she had a right to the same from him, well, that was different. He didn't trust, not her, but his own emotions. Overburdened, he cupped his hands over his mouth and called for Brent. He heard something he took as a response, but the boy wasn't yet in sight which meant he'd have to spend more time with Kristen.

"You're right," he heard her say. "We both know better. At least we should."

Joe wasn't sure he knew anything except that he needed to keep his distance if he didn't want things to go beyond the point of no return, if he didn't want his deepest emotions ripped open.

"From now on," she continued, her voice small, "the only time we'll see each other is when it concerns Brent. Is that the way you want it?"

"Look, I can't pretend I don't know what I do about you."

"I guess that's my problem, isn't it," she said, now sounding both strong and hurt.

"I wish you wouldn't call it that. Look, there aren't any guidelines for what we're doing. By the way, we're going to need to talk about what's best for that Andy kid," he said in the take-charge tone that got him through his workday. "I want you to take a look at my liability insurance so—"

"Not tonight, Joe," she interrupted. "I'll turn into a social worker again on Monday but this weekend I'm a mother."

A mother who was raising her daughter alone because her ex-husband couldn't be trusted to fulfill his role—just as he'd once done.

"I don't want to lose touch with Susanna," he admitted without wisdom.

"You just met her."

"She needs a father in her life."

"What my daughter does or doesn't need is my concern, not yours." Before he could say anything, she'd turned her back and marched away. He let her go.

Sunday with his father had been a disaster, Joe admitted. Not only had Brent radiated hostility throughout the visit, but his father had talked endlessly about his dead wife. Joe had suggested at least three times that his father visit the relatives still living in California; his father had no interest in such a populated state and added that he didn't want to get on a plane when he'd done so twice and hadn't enjoyed it. At least on the way home Brent had made the observation that it was hard for a man to lose his wife after a lifetime of living together, making Joe hopeful that the boy was capable of putting himself in another person's position.

That, in a way, was what was happening today. Although he didn't want to visit his sister in jail before she was sent to wherever she'd spend the duration of her imprisonment, she deserved to see her son and Brent needed the same connection.

When he started debating the pros and cons of the meeting, he'd considered running it past Kristen, but what had happened at the rodeo still left him feeling out of control. Besides, he couldn't remember the last time he'd had to consult anyone before making a decision. Kristen Childers might have placed Brent with him, but the boy was his nephew and Hannah his sister.

He'd tried to prepare Brent for the reality of having to sit across from his mother while guards looked on, but obviously this was the last place the boy wanted to be. Still, he had to hand it to him; he'd left his anger and fear at the front door and was concentrating on what his mother was saying.

"I didn't see as I had any choice. They found all this evidence against me so what was the point of going to trial?" Hannah said. "My lawyer—all he cared was that I don't take too much of his time 'cause he had this big case he was working on."

"Why didn't you ask for a different attorney?" he asked.

She picked at the sleeve of her overlarge orange jumpsuit. "When you don't have no money, the lawyers aren't exactly beating a path to your door."

"You could have asked me."

"No, I couldn't, bro. I screwed up, big time." Closing her eyes, she nodded. Hannah looked older than the last time he'd seen her and not once had Joe heard the self-pitying tone that used to set him on edge. "Even if you'd bought me decent defense, it wouldn't have changed anything."

She might not have made a public confession, but he knew her well enough to understand the meaning behind her words and suspected Brent did too. The boy hadn't said much but then his mother had done little to include him in the conversation. In fact, other than telling Brent he needed a haircut, she'd barely acknowledged his presence.

"Then you've resigned yourself to what's happening?" he asked.

"What choice do I have? The system's got me."

But the system wasn't the villain here, Joe knew. "Do me a favor, will you?"

"Like what? My options are kinda limited."

He leaned forward to assure that she concentrated on him. "I asked. You can get your GED while you're serving your time."

"School?" she snorted. "You know how I feel about that."

"I swallowed my pride and admitted to my ignorance," he pointed out. "Went back for the education I should have gotten a long time before. I'm asking you to do the same thing, if not for yourself, for your son."

Hannah's attention briefly flickered to Brent. "I'll think about it."

"Uncle Joe, why bother?" Brent demanded. "You're not going to change her."

"I'm not asking her to remake herself." The gray walls in the too-small room seemed to absorb most of the day's sunlight. If it was him trapped in here, he wasn't sure he'd remain sane, but his sister seemed unaware of her depressing surroundings. "I'm just asking her to make something good come out of this."

"What about it, Mom?" Brent asked. "You want to have a race to see which of us graduates from high school first?"

"Don't you use that smart mouth around me!"

Brent stood so suddenly that his chair nearly tipped over. "I was trying to make a joke, Mom. Why do I try? You tell me, why did I bother to come here?"

"I didn't ask you to."

"No, you didn't." Pain lapped at the edge of Brent's words. "You get to use a phone, don't you? You knew where I was. Why didn't you at least call me?"

"I had a lot on my mind."

He reached out but didn't touch his mother. "Why did you have me if I'm such an inconvenience?" he asked. Not bothering to wait for an answer, Brent hurried toward the door and impatiently waited for the guard to open it for him.

Sensing Brent needed time alone with his emotions, Joe remained where he was. Hannah was a little more than a year older than him, but he wondered if he knew her at all. Kristen Childers, a woman he'd known only a couple of weeks, was more accessible, her emotions cleaner.

"He's got my temper," Hannah observed wearily. "Fat lot of good it's going to do him."

"He's got a right to be angry."

"What are you doing, taking his side?"

"No, I'm not. But there is one thing I'd like to know."

His sister watched him the way a trapped animal might study the setter of that trap.

"Why did you say so little to him? He's your son. Don't you care about him?"

Hannah's features had hardened so long ago that he had to look at old photographs to remember that she'd once embraced life. Now, however, he saw a glimpse of the energetic child she had been before alcohol and helplessness had got the better of her. Her chin trembled and she pushed at her long, limp hair with a less than steady hand.

"I'm no good for him, bro," she whispered. "Never was, and getting an education behind bars ain't going to change things."

"He needs a parent, Hannah."

"You shoulda taken him away from me a long time ago." Hannah, his tough sister, was on the brink of tears.

"I messed up my opportunity for that, remember," he reminded her. Not caring how the guards would react, he rested his hands on her shoulders. "I worry about you."

"I can take care of myself. Always have and always will. But . . ."

"What?"

"Joe, I'm no good for him."

His very words to Kristen when she first asked him to include his nephew in his life, Joe remembered with a pang. "It doesn't have to be that way," he told Hannah. "If you'd just get your act together—"

"It's too late. Bro, it's going to be at least three years before they let me out. He'll be a teenager by then, the same age you and I were when we started getting in trouble. I know—the thought of being responsible for him scares me to death."

Although he understood why Hannah felt the way

she did, it bothered him that, as usual, her thoughts were focused on herself and not her son.

"I can't do it," she whispered.

"You're giving up?"

"I don't care what you call it. I mean it. I'm no good for him. But you are."

"I'm trying."

"Raise him, please!" She moved as if to stand, then collapsed with her elbows on the table and her head cupped in her hands. "Give him what I can't."

"Hannah, you don't know—"

"I do! I want you to adopt him. That way I know he'll be safe."

TEN

Kristen was listening with half an ear to her voice-mail messages when her breath caught. "I'm going to be in your part of town this afternoon," Joe had said. "If you've got time to see me, there's something we need to discuss."

It was afternoon, which meant Joe could show up any time. Instead of dealing with the other demands on her time, she hurried into the restroom and checked her image in the mirror. She'd worn cream-colored slacks and a white blouse which was now a little wrinkled but didn't look that bad. When she dug through her purse for lipstick, she carefully didn't ask herself what she was doing; what mattered was that she'd be seeing Joe for the first time in three days.

She'd no more than sat back down in her chair when the receptionist buzzed to let her know someone was here to see her, and although the two small meeting rooms were being used, no one was in the conference room in case she wanted to take her client in there.

"Where did you find him?" the receptionist whispered. "What a hunk."

"Jeannie!"

"Don't worry. He can't hear me. I repeat, where did you find him?"

"It's a long story."

"Please tell me he isn't married." Not quite twenty-one, Jeannie's sole purpose in life seemed to be critiquing Roswell's male population.

"He isn't married."

"You lucky dog," Jeannie continued in her low, conspiratorial tone. "Look, I'd better not catch the two of you alone in a closed room. However, if it was me . . ."

Joe was standing when she poked her head into the reception room. Tall and proud, he looked out of place in the room with boxes filled with toys, battered plastic chairs, and posters warning of the dangers of child abuse. Several people were waiting to be seen and Jeannie was watching everything, but all she could think about was that she'd kissed Joe Red Shadow the other night.

"I wasn't sure you'd be in," he said once they were in the large, empty conference room. Despite Jeannie's warnings, she'd closed the door behind him. "I was taking a chance."

"I'm glad I got back in time. Ah, air conditioning." She made a show of letting the unit blow on her so she wouldn't have to face Joe until she'd calmed down a little. "The AC in the state car never has a chance to cool off the interior because I'm in and out so much. I'd think it would be all but impossible for you to work in the afternoon."

"I'm used to it."

Of course he was. Besides, he hadn't come here to listen to her chatter about the weather. She sat in one of the chairs pulled up around the large table, but instead of sitting opposite her, he settled himself next to her. "What is this about?" she asked.

"Business."

Yes, business. Of course. That's what they'd agreed their relationship would be about from now on.

"I took Brent to see his mother the other day," he said without preamble. "She and I had a short but important conversation."

"You did?" Kristen started to say, then the first part of his announcement sank in. "You took Brent to the jail?"

"Yes."

"Without consulting me?"

"Consulting you?" If there'd been anything soft and warm in his voice, it no longer existed. "He's my nephew. I don't have to get your permission every time I turn around."

"It's not like that and you know it. A jail?"

"He has a right and a need to see his mother. Since that's where she is, I didn't have much choice."

She'd been at loggerheads with clients before, knew what it was like to be yelled at, even called vile names. In no way was this confrontation with Joe like that, and yet lines had been drawn between them. Even as her professionalism kicked in, she said a regretful good-bye to what they'd briefly shared.

"Joe, Brent is a ward of the state and as a representative of that state, I'm responsible for making certain decisions in his interest. I thought you understood that, and that you knew which situations warranted discussing them with me first."

When he leaned back, his chair groaned. His beautiful black eyes still touched her nerve endings, but if she'd had any doubt of his ability to face life head-on, she no longer did. "You sound like a bureaucrat," he told her. "Like you're reading out of a manual. What is it? They drum rules and regulations into you until that's all you can spout?"

"Wait a minute. That isn't—"

"Isn't it? I want to talk about my nephew, not some ward of the state." Folding his arms across his chest, he stared at her for a long time before continuing.

"We're more than social worker and whatever the hell people like you call me. In case you've forgotten, I put your daughter on my horse and you watched me ride and rope and we—"

"I know what we did," she interrupted. "It shouldn't have happened."

That elicited a shrug from him. "Maybe. Maybe not. What we can't do is pretend it didn't happen. That's why I thought you'd be willing to work with me, tell me what I need to do next."

A faint squeak outside told her that someone was walking down the hall. She waited to see if that person was going to poke his or her head inside, then concentrated all her attention on Joe. There was no denying it; he remained the most arresting man she'd ever known.

"What you need to do?" she asked when maybe she should have insisted they stay on the issue of the unauthorized jail visit.

"Yeah."

His eyes became unfocused, and she guessed he was reaching inside himself. Jeannie was right; he was a hunk. What the receptionist didn't know was how much more there was to him.

"Hannah wants me to adopt Brent."

Of all the things he could have said, that was the

last she expected. Trying to keep her mouth from opening in surprise, she concentrated on the placement of her fingers under her chin. She had the suspicion she looked like a wise owl when she didn't feel wise at all.

"Adopt," she whispered, then berated herself for mindlessly echoing him.

He nodded. "She might change her mind, but I don't think so. I've thought about it a lot. At first I considered simply becoming his legal guardian, but he's never had much security and I can offer him that by showing him that I want him to be part of my life in every way possible."

"Adoption's a complicated process," she said. "You'd have to get Hannah's formal agreement and secure the same thing from Brent's father."

"I know."

"There'd be a lot of red tape."

"I know."

"And it can be expensive."

"Are you trying to discourage me?"

No, she started to say, but it was more complex than that. Joe was running on emotion; she understood that and wanted to be part of that emotion, but it was her job to root him in reality. She'd done so before when foster parents sought to adopt the children in their care. What made it different this time was that she'd begun to understand Joe as a human being and—

Who was she kidding? What she felt for this man went beyond what she'd felt for anyone she'd dealt with on or off the job.

"We're a long way from being able to even discuss that," Kristen told him. "In case you've forgotten, you only have him on a temporary basis. Until your background check has been completed and you've been approved—"

"What is this, a bank loan?"

"Of course not. Joe, I wouldn't be doing my job if I didn't play devil's advocate. It wouldn't be fair if I didn't make you aware of all the negative—"

"I know what you're doing." When he stood, he did it so smoothly that for several seconds the change didn't register. Stepping over to her, he leaned forward. "Believe me, I'm very aware of how the system works. In case you've forgotten, I have a daughter who doesn't live under the same roof as me. As a result, I've gone the whole child support route."

"Then you know—"

"Don't try to tell me what I know."

What had happened to the man she'd stood in front of as night claimed the rodeo grounds? That man had been gentle mystery and promise, not intimidating the way he was now.

"I want Brent. It's what's best for him and his mother agrees. All this other stuff"—he waved his arm as if encompassing the entire building—"has nothing to do with those simple facts."

Joe was wrong, so wrong, but this wasn't the time to try to make him fully comprehend the hold her agency had over him. If it was within her power, she'd fling open the door and scream at him to run for freedom. She would even be tempted to join him in that headlong dash. However, that wasn't possible.

"Doesn't it?" she asked, hating herself. He still loomed over her and she was forced to look up at him, her awareness of his size and essence growing with every breath she took.

"Joe, you took Brent to a place of incarceration without first gaining permission."

"He and his mother have a right to see each other."

He was never going to change his mind on that; why was she trying? "When I first approached you, you said you weren't any good for him."

That silenced him. He continued to stare at her as if trying to dig a hole through her, and his body was now so tight and tense that she wondered if it might shatter.

"I wish you hadn't told me that," Kristen admitted, unable to lift her voice above a whisper. "I wish I could forget those words, but I can't."

"And you refuse to go beyond them, don't you?"

That wasn't the response she needed, but she did what she could with it. However, before answering, she scooted back and stood up, trying to make the movement casual.

"First reactions can be the most honest ones," she told him. "My job has taught me to pay special attention to what people say and do before they've had time to get their defenses up."

"And was what you did the other night before or after you'd gotten your defenses in place?"

"We're not talking about that," she managed.

"Aren't we?"

Joe let his body do his talking for him. His dusty boots made only the faintest whisper of sound as he stepped toward her. His arms went around her, gently trapping her own arms by her side, and when he lowered his head toward her, it was in question, not demand. She could have said no; her body could have ordered him away.

However, it didn't. Instead, she tilted her chin upward, and her mouth parted. His kiss, while not bruising, left no doubt of how much he wanted her. In a disjointed way, she understood how little control he had over what they were doing, and she knew she should have been the one to drag them back to sanity. But when her eyes closed, nothing remained except him.

The electricity between them awakened her flesh, and she felt a sensual warmth deep within her. Surely she wasn't returning his kiss with the same intensity he was giving, but a powerful force had taken hold of her and the hunger in her demanded to be satisfied. Her sensitized lips felt and took of him, tasting and making that taste part of her. Beneath the softness of his mouth was strength and in a way she couldn't begin to understand, softness and strength flowed together, becoming one.

It was dangerous for them to have been alone so long. She'd thought herself safe because she'd denied her sexual nature all these years, but she'd been wrong. Like a wild creature kept too long in confinement, she now craved life. Craved the feel of a man's arms around her and his mouth promising more—only not just any man would do.

"Joe?" she mouthed. "Joe." His name was the only word she knew at that moment.

"I know," he whispered. "I know."

When it seemed as if he might pull away, she slid her arms around his waist and pressed the side of her head against his chest where his heart beat. A fundamental part of the training for her job had been the warning not to have anything of a personal nature to do with a client. True, they were on the same side of the situation instead of him being someone the agency had an adversarial relationship with, but that didn't make things any less fraught with danger.

In the end, what gave her the strength to break away was her insecurities when it came to men. With a little cry, she drew back and after a moment, turned her back on him and half-walked, half-stumbled to the door. Joe didn't say anything and neither did she. No matter how carefully she might choose her words, they'd reveal too much. It took all her strength not to reach for him once more.

Back at her desk, Kristen tried to bury herself in paperwork, but her mind kept flitting to what had happened a few minutes before. Time and time again her cheeks flamed, not so much with embarrassment, but with a landslide of emotions. She hadn't done her job. He'd come to her with a request for guidance but instead of giving him the benefit of her experience, she'd forgotten who she was and had allowed emotion to take over. Along with everything else she now felt, she was disappointed in herself.

Gradually she became aware that someone was standing at the entrance to her cubicle. "What was that about?" her supervisor asked.

"What was what about?" She acknowledged Bob Cogswell with what she hoped was a casual glance. If only she'd had the presence of mind to check her appearance in a mirror.

"I was walking past the conference room when I heard your voice and someone else's. Whatever the conversation was about, it sounded pretty intense. I checked and found out that you were meeting with that Apache foster parent."

Thank goodness Bob believed in allowing his workers to do their jobs. Otherwise, he might have walked into the room. Because she needed to run at least some of what had happened past someone who could be objective, she told him that Joe wanted to adopt his nephew.

"He took the boy to the jail?" Bob asked. "Without clearing it with you first?"

"He's Brent's uncle," she started, then stopped because that had been the very argument Joe had used with her. "But no," she amended. "He didn't."

"What was his reaction when you called him on it?"

"He didn't like it." Her face still felt flushed and she couldn't keep her hands still.

"Then that's what the argument was about?"

It had been more complex than that, but she merely nodded.

"I hate to say it, but from what I heard, it didn't sound as if you were making much headway in getting him to see the agency's side of things. Look, Kristen, you're good at your job, but that doesn't mean you should try to work with everyone who walks through the door. If you want another worker assigned to the case—"

"No!" she blurted. "I mean, I know the situation and I believe Brent trusts me . . ." After a few seconds of tight silence, she finished by reassuring Bob that she was determined to seeing Brent's placement through to a satisfactory conclusion. She had, she reminded Bob, dealt with volatile people in the past and would continue to do so as completely as she knew how.

"It's your decision," he said as he turned to leave. "But back when we were getting the new day care program going, I attended several planning commission meetings Red Shadow was at. The man doesn't back down from anything."

Alone with her supervisor's words echoing around her, Kristen agreed. But she knew all too well that Joe was much more than a potential adversary. No matter how impossible, how dangerous and insane it was to think such a thing, she wanted him to be her lover.

ELEVEN

Andy Pilimar fiddled with his seatbelt while he chattered about the movie he'd seen last night. Every time the retarded young man paused for breath, Kristen tried to bring his thoughts around to the way he'd have to conduct himself if he hoped to have a job Mescalero Apache Construction, but Andy had loved the movie's fights and car crashes too much to concentrate on anything else. At least listening to him kept her from focusing entirely on what seeing Joe again would do to her nervous system. They'd only spoken once since he'd come to her office yesterday and that had been to settle on a time to bring Andy out.

Joe was waiting outside the trailer which served as his office. All but ignoring her, he shook hands with Andy, introduced himself, and got down to business at once. He told Andy how important it was that tools be properly cared for and material not remain scattered. He'd have someone show Andy where to stack wood, cinder blocks, bags of cement, metal, and other items.

"You use saws, don't you?" Andy asked, his eyes big as he studied a forklift that was slowly moving past them. "I want to sharpen saws."

She wondered if Joe might dismiss that out of hand, but he only said that he first wanted to see what kind of care Andy took of the hammers, staple guns, routers, and other equipment. Andy nodded agreement, but Kristen wasn't sure how much he heard because he never took his eyes off the forklift. Smiling a little, Joe called to the lift operator and asked him to show Andy how it worked. As soon as Andy understood what was happening, he loped toward it.

"What do you think?" she asked. "I know his special ed teacher is convinced he can follow commands and is responsible, but—"

"I'll give it a shot, Kristen."

She wished he wouldn't speak her name because whenever he did, the only thing she could concentrate on was the way he made it sound. "I know you will," she replied. "And I hope you realize how grateful the agency is that you're willing to do this."

"I'm not doing it for the agency."

Instantly on the alert—not that she hadn't been before—she gazed up at him. Because the sun was behind him, she had to squint and his features remained indistinct. Just the same, she didn't need to look into his eyes to remember everything she'd learned about them.

"I'd ask you into my office"—he indicated the trailer—"but there's hardly room to turn around and we both know what happens when we're in confined spaces together."

"Joe," she warned, her cheeks instantly flushed. "Today isn't about that."

"Isn't it? All right. It isn't, at least not now. You're drawing a lot of attention, but since there's nowhere private we can go, I guess you'll have to put up with it."

She was vaguely aware of casual and some not so casual glances, but Joe had a smudge on the side of his neck, and she couldn't think about anything except taking a cloth to it and gently rubbing his flesh.

"Come on," he said roughly. "Let's walk."

Kristen didn't move until he cupped his fingers around her elbow and began to lead her to the rear of the emerging buildings. She gave a belated thought to Andy, but he was obviously in seventh heaven as a middle-aged man pointed out something about the forklift's giant tires. Joe wouldn't have left Andy in just anyone's care, and if he trusted the older man, so could she.

"I mean it," she said once Joe was no longer holding onto her, "about being grateful that you're taking a chance on Andy. He needs his self-confidence boosted, but it isn't easy finding the proper workplace for that to happen."

"I hope it works out," he replied, then stopped.

Back here, some of the stacks of material waiting to be put to use towered over her head. Massive metal bars at least twenty feet in length had been placed in a number of rows, and Joe had taken them between those rows. "W-what—" She took a deep breath before continuing. "What do you mean, you hope things work out? Joe, if you have doubts, please tell me."

"What I'm saying is, I can't look into the future any more than anyone else."

That made sense, making her sorry she'd questioned him. Although she'd already given him a rundown on the phone of what Andy's teachers thought he could accomplish, she gave him a quick update.

Even with her constant awareness of Joe as a man, she enjoyed talking to him this way.

"I can't help thinking how things have changed for the mentally challenged," she wound up. "Not many years ago he would have been warehoused in an institution or his family left alone to raise him."

"You're right." Joe's thoughtful smile said he agreed totally. "But you do understand I'm not going to be able to spend much time with him, don't you? I've asked my senior foreman to show him the ropes, but we run a business here, not a sheltered workshop."

"Yes, I understand." She took a chance on touching his forearm. He looked down but gave no other reaction which prompted her to continue. "Do you feel pressured into this?" she asked. "Perhaps you wouldn't have considered it if the request hadn't come from me."

"No, that's not it." He leaned against the nearest stack, then sighed. "Kristen, there are a few things you need to know. I debated telling you, but I think you need everything laid out."

"I-I appreciate that."

"When I first started this business, all I thought about was whether I'd be able to make a go of it. It turned out better than I thought it would, but that didn't take the pressure off, only turned it in another direction."

Kristen only nodded.

"It's the responsibility," he said. "The responsibility for so many people that keeps me awake nights."

"I guess you lose a lot of sleep."

"Sometimes." He gave her a rueful grin. "Just after I got the contract for this job, I thought insomnia was going to do me in."

"I'm sorry."

"It goes with the territory. All these people"—he gestured, taking in their surroundings—"have families to support, bills to pay. To some extent, what they're going to be able to do with their lives rests on my ability to run this construction business well."

She had to agree, but she knew how much it all weighed on him. "Do you ever wish you'd done something different with your life?"

"Other than becoming a professional rodeo cowboy, which I realized was a stupid, juvenile pipe dream the first time I broke a bone, this is the only thing I've wanted to do."

Honesty was his watchword, and along with it he had an openness that she found rare and precious. "So, you've learned to live with all the responsibilities that go with it. I applaud you."

"Just don't expect me to be a miracle worker."

"I won't." She wondered if they were talking about more than Andy. "Joe, I was naive when I went into social work. I had this idea that because I'd been able to pull my life together after my divorce, that it would be easy to show others how to do the same thing. I was wrong."

"That can't be easy to admit."

"It's reality." It was her turn to smile. "If someone who's been referred to our agency gets their lives straightened out, it's because they had what it took inside them, not because I or one of my co-workers has worked a miracle."

"And if your whatever you call them—"

"Clients."

"If your clients fail, it's not your fault."

"Yes," she admitted. "Although sometimes that's hard for me to accept."

"It's the same as when I have to let people go because they aren't doing their job."

There were a million things she could share with him, but she didn't believe anything more needed to be said. She and her co-workers often talked about the limitations and frustrations of their jobs along with the successes, but with everything she and Joe were and weren't to each other, their shared revelations were nothing short of amazing.

"I have to go," he told her. "But I hope you understand now I'm not making any predictions where Andy is concerned."

"I do."

"Yes. You do. And Kristen, thank you for telling me what you did."

If she didn't command her legs to walk, he was going to leave her behind, but she was content to study his retreating back. There were so many layers to Joe Red Shadow that she doubted she'd ever discover all of them. From the moment she'd met him, she'd experienced a sexual attraction of a strength that left her almost speechless at times. She might have been content to focus on sensual awareness, but there'd been so much more to him and sometimes, like now, she needed to touch and be touched by his mind instead of his hands and body.

"Kristen? Are you coming?"

"Yes," she said, and caught up easily because he'd slowed to wait for her. "Joe, do you talk to anyone about the pressure of being responsible for so many people?"

"Talk? No."

"Why not?"

That gave him momentary pause. "The men and women under me don't need to hear it, and I'm not about to reveal something like that to financial backers or planners."

"So you hold it inside. The reason I asked, well, I can grouse to my co-workers."

Reaching out, she took his hand, and although her strength could never match his, maybe he could take something from her. When he returned her squeeze, she told herself she'd succeeded. They were no longer touching by the time the sights and sounds and smells of construction once again assaulted her, but somehow she knew he wasn't done speaking.

"You're good at what you do," Joe told her. "Empathetic and understanding."

"Thank you. And you're good at what you do."

"So what are we?" he asked in a teasing tone. "A mutual admiration society?"

"I hope we understand each other more than we did before. Joe, I hope we can always be honest with each other."

"I hope so too."

During the next two days, most of Kristen's time was taken up with testifying in two juvenile court cases, but whenever the phone rang, she hoped it would be Joe. It wasn't, and what little she heard about him came from Andy's father. He informed her proudly that Andy loved building buildings, as he put it, and thought his boss was the greatest thing since sliced bread. Sam Che at the Apache tribal council called to ask if she had any updates on Joe's background investigation, which prompted her to again request a police check from Nevada. On Friday she managed to be at the school in time to give Brent a ride out to the work site.

"You know what I'm going to ask," she told him once she'd learned that he'd been invited to spend Saturday night at a new friend's house. "How are things going between you and your uncle?"

"Fine. No sweat."

"Are you learning anything working with him? Do you think it might become a kind of apprenticeship program?"

"Maybe once school's out. Electricians are the ones who really make the money. I sure wouldn't mind doing that."

Pleased Brent was thinking in terms of a career, she asked if he'd had any contact with his mother and was told that Hannah had written a couple of letters but they'd been pretty short.

"I'm sorry," she said. She considered bringing up what Joe and she had discussed about his wanting to adopt Brent but didn't. Instead, she told him that her daughter insisted on hearing an Apache legend every night.

"Well, I don't have a choice," Brent muttered. "I get them rammed down my throat."

"What would you prefer your uncle do, wait until you ask on your own?"

"Like I'm going to? Look, I never did buy into fairytales, and being part Apache is no big deal. The thing is, the more I try to back off, the harder he pushes. It's a royal drag."

Because they'd reached the site and Brent had already opened the door, even if she'd known what to say, time was running short.

"Do you want me to talk to him about it?" she asked.

"I don't care. It's probably good I'm going to be gone most of the weekend and he's riding in that race. That way there won't be time for us to get into it again."

When Kristen got home that evening, there was a message from her parents asking if Susanna could spend Saturday with them. Her mother mentioned a new children's movie out that sounded interesting, and they didn't want to embarrass themselves by going to it without a child in tow. As she expected, Susanna was all for it.

By the time she'd confirmed arrangements with her parents and had thrown together an easy dinner, all she wanted to do was relax. As her daughter settled down in front of the TV, she picked up the newspaper. Although she felt guilty because she knew so little about what had been going on in the world lately, she turned to the sports page. She read it carefully until she found the small article about a horse race being held at the rodeo grounds Saturday night. It was set to begin at 7 p.m.

Clouds had moved in from the west which had lowered the temperature a few degrees. Because desert nights could be cool, Kristen had brought along a light windbreaker. Most of the audience consisted of families or couples and she felt out of place until she spotted the older couple she'd sat beside before and they invited her to join them.

"I wondered if we'd see you again," the woman admitted. "Interested in Joe, are you?"

"It's not—" she started but couldn't finish. "A little, maybe," she admitted.

"Good for you. And if you're here to check him out when he doesn't suspect, so much the better. The way I figure it, the more a woman knows about a man, the better."

The woman's husband snorted at that, then reminded her that after forty-six years of marriage, he was the only man she knew anything about and that wasn't much. Kristen shared their good-natured laughter, then allowed her attention to wander. She was here, she'd told herself as she was getting ready, because it was important to Brent's future that she learn everything she possibly could about the man who wanted to adopt him. He'd been called wild. If that part of his nature came out tonight—

Who was she fooling? It was Saturday night and she'd come to watch an exciting man.

The arena's basic structure hadn't changed, but a chalk and traffic cone racecourse had been laid out close to the fence. Because the arena wasn't that large, she surmised that the ability to execute close turns was more important than speed. As she watched a couple of riders taking their horses through their paces, a vague unease settled into her. Joe's horse—if he used the same mare he had the other night—was trained for quick stops, starts, and turns and Joe had spent much of his life on horseback, but there was no guaranteeing what others might do.

"How many horses are in each race?" she asked.

"It depends. Tonight's a good field. We might get twenty at some of the shorter runs."

Twenty? Although that didn't seem to bother the older couple, she couldn't imagine that many horses jockeying for the same limited space. She wanted to inquire if riders were ever injured but couldn't bring herself to ask the question.

No less than five novices had signed up for tonight's events. Joe heard grumbling from some of the other seasoned riders, but although he agreed, he didn't add his argument to theirs.

Something, maybe the clouds, had put him in a pensive mood. Things had been a little strained between him and Brent as the boy hurried through his chores so he could leave, and he'd been grateful both for the silence after his nephew had gone and the fact that he had something physical to do tonight.

He'd considered asking Kristen if she and her daughter wanted to watch him, but given what had happened during their last couple of meetings, distance was the wiser option. Besides, she probably would have turned him down. Why, he wondered as the gelding he'd bought last fall pranced and snorted in response to other horses' nervousness, did his relationship with her have to be so complicated; even more than that, why couldn't he get her out of his system?

"You ready for this?" Ralph Running Deer asked as the tall, skinny man joined him. "I swear, it looks like kindergarten around here tonight. The newcomers get younger all the time."

"Tell me about it," Joe agreed. Then, although one of the novices was barely able to remain astride his undisciplined mount, he worked his gelding into position next to it.

As the starting pistol blasted, the newcomer's horse reared and a flailing front hoof caught his gelding a glancing blow. Although he managed to keep New Blue under control, they were half a beat behind the leaders before he could get underway. Leaning low along New Blue's neck, he whispered encouragement. Before they'd circled the arena once, they were running neck and neck with Ralph and a couple of other experienced racers.

Ralph's horse took the inside turn too tightly and bumped the horse next to the fence. Taking advantage of the confusion, Joe guided New Blue around them. He'd aimed New Blue into the next straight stretch when he sensed something coming up too fast behind him. Glancing over his shoulder, he saw that the horse that had struck New Blue at the beginning was riderless, a mindless terror showing in the animal's rolling eyes.

"Damn!" Reining New Blue sharply to the right, he gave the panicking horse room to run past. Unfortunately, just as he was neck and neck with New Blue, the runaway wheeled and slammed into him.

Squealing, New Blue struggled to keep his legs under him. He might have succeeded if the two horses' legs hadn't tangled. Joe was aware of many things all at once: the smell of horse sweat, hooves thudding on packed earth, gasps from the crowd, New Blue being knocked to the side. In the second before it happened, Joe knew he was going to be thrown. Releasing the reins, he managed to throw up an arm to protect his face. Then his shoulder, followed by his arms, hip, and legs, slammed into the fence. His head snapped back and then everything went black.

TWELVE

Kristen was on her feet in an instant. A few other members of the audience had stood up as the collision unfolded but most remained seated, probably because this wasn't the first time they'd seen such an accident.

Her eyes remained fixed on the tangle of horses and man. The riderless horse was the first to get up and after shaking its entire body as if trying to rid itself of its saddle and bridle, it galloped to the center of the arena where it ran in tight circles. Joe's mount was slower to stand. Although she could tell that it was trembling, it remained where it was, proof, she suspected, of how well it had been trained.

Now she could see Joe, but he was so far away that all she knew about his condition was that he hadn't moved.

"It's all right, honey," the elderly woman reassured her. "He's been thrown before and there's always a couple of emergency medical technicians at these events. Just you watch. He'll be getting up any time now."

But he wasn't. For a horrible minute, she thought the other horses were going to run over Joe when they came around the track for the second time, but the riders must have all seen what had happened because, almost as one, they slowed their mounts and rode in a wide arc around Joe. By then several men had emerged from behind the arena and were hurrying toward him. He lay motionless in the dirt.

"Wait!" the woman called out, but it was too late because Kristen was already making her way down the steps and frantically looking around for a way to reach Joe.

People backed up to let her pass, and one man pointed to the rear of the bleachers, reminding her that this was the route she'd taken when she'd gone behind the chutes the other time she'd been here. Joe couldn't be hurt! He couldn't!

Although it seemed to take forever, she finally made her way to the gate which served as the entrance to the arena and was both relieved and frightened to see that a group of men and women had gathered and that they were all looking down at something—or someone. Breathless, she stopped and wrapped her arms tight around herself. She had no business being here. These people would take care of Joe and she'd only be in the way. She'd make herself turn around and walk back. . . .

But how could she until she knew whether he was all right?

"Don't you be trying to sit up," a deep-voiced man ordered. "Talk about a hard head. Joe, you have no idea—"

"Listen to him, you fool," someone else interrupted. "Damn it, Joe, take a look at that knot on your shoulder."

He was alive! Alive and that's all that mattered. Not caring what others might think, she worked her way into the group until she spotted two men kneeling on the ground on either side of Joe who lay with his legs outstretched and one arm folded over his chest. One of the kneelers was taking his pulse.

"Joe?" That frightened whisper couldn't be coming from her, could it? "Joe, are you all right?"

"Kristen?"

Denims were for rugged use, but even if she'd been wearing silk, that wouldn't have stopped her from dropping down beside Joe. She couldn't remember when she'd started to shake, not that it mattered, for the simple reason that he'd spoken her name. Someone had removed his shirt and although it was night and the lighting poor, she could see a large welt on his left shoulder.

"What happened?" Only once she heard herself did she realize how inane the question was.

"Lost an argument with a fence," Joe answered, a wan smile briefly touching his lips. "I didn't know you were here."

That wasn't important. Nothing was except seeing him standing tall and healthy again. However, although she had to quell an impulse to pull him to his feet, she forced herself to scoot back a little so the paramedics could finish checking him out. Fortunately, she soon learned that he'd sustained no head injuries or cuts and hadn't been stepped on. However, he'd been right in his assessment that he'd lost an argument with a fence because one man informed everyone within earshot that Joe was going to be one bruised cowboy for a few days.

By then Joe was sitting up. He listened closely to what the paramedics were saying but every once in awhile, his attention flickered to her, his eyes asking silent questions.

I'm here, she answered in the same way. *Please don't ask me to explain why.*

A number of hands reached out to help Joe to his feet. Although he favored his right leg, he showed no sign of collapsing. One of the other riders, an Indian whom Joe called Ralph, told him that New Blue was being loaded into Joe's trailer. Because Joe's truck was an older model with standard shift and no power steering, Ralph was offering to drive it. Joe could either go with him or travel with the other cowboy who'd agreed to give Ralph a ride home from Joe's place.

"If you want to be checked out at the hospital first," Ralph concluded, "I'll take care of New Blue. Whatever you decide, don't worry about the gelding."

"Joe's coming home with me," Kristen heard herself say.

"I'm what?" A hint of something that might have been amusement lit his dark eyes.

"You're spending the night with me," she told Joe finally. "You shouldn't be alone."

What in the world had gotten into her, Kristen thought a half hour later as she unlocked the door to her second story apartment and stepped back to let Joe in. They hadn't said much during the ride home beyond a brief rehash of the accident. He blamed himself for what had happened, repeating that he knew how excitable horses were, even when she tried to point out he couldn't possibly have gotten New Blue out of the other animal's way. She'd bring it up again in the morning, maybe. Now, however, she had all she could do to accept the simple fact that Joe Red Shadow was standing in the middle of her no-nonsense living room. She'd told him that Susanna was spending the night with her parents, but if he'd read anything into that, he wasn't saying. Instead, she had the uneasy feeling that although he handled himself as if every muscle ached, he was learning a great deal about her from what her place revealed.

"Cliff left me with a lot of bills," she explained. "I've gotten them all cleared up, but it didn't leave anything for furniture. Besides, saving money for a down payment on a house is a lot more important than couches and chairs."

Maybe it was the mention of a chair that drew first his attention and then his body to the tan recliner she'd picked up at a yard sale. He gritted his teeth as he sat down, then leaned his head back and briefly closed his eyes.

"I'm getting too old for this nonsense," he muttered. "Maybe it's time I stopped thinking of myself as a kid."

"You're hardly that," Kristen told him, her eyes not leaving his long, lean frame. He'd slipped back into his shirt but hadn't bothered with buttons, and when he sat down, it had fallen open, revealing too much. Strange, she thought, as a mixture of cold and heat chased each other through her; a touch of nudity can be just as exciting as the whole thing.

His chest moved up and down, up and down. She nearly asked if he wanted her to engage the footrest but if she did, she might be tempted to help him out of his boots or remove the silver and leather belt from around his waist and she wasn't yet brave or reckless enough for that. Joe Red Shadow was in her apartment. He was going to spend the night.

Mouth dry, she asked if he'd like a couple of aspirin.

He started to shake his head, and she thought he was going to say no, but with a grimace, he said he'd appreciate it. She hurried through the small task of selecting the aspirin and getting him a drink of water, then hesitated at the opening between kitchen and living room. His eyes were half-closed, his body looking more relaxed than it had when he'd first sat down.

"Thank you," he said. He hadn't looked at her which made her wonder if he'd been able to sense her presence. "You didn't have to do this."

"I know." Stepping into the room, she walked over to him and handed him the pills and water.

"Why did you?"

"I don't know," she admitted. "I saw you get hurt and suddenly nothing mattered except getting to you. Then when I realized you might have no one to care for you tonight . . ."

"Go on Kristen. Finish what you were going to say."

"I-I knew I didn't want that for you."

The pain pills must have been exactly what his system needed because not more than ten minutes after he'd taken them, Joe felt himself begin to fall asleep. He'd arranged for Brent to stay with a buddy and told his nephew where he was. Then Kristen insisted he use her bed. His argument that he didn't want to put her out fell away when she informed him that she would be perfectly comfortable in Susanna's room and then began to pull off his boots. Once she was done doing that, her eyes had strayed to his belt, but much as he might have liked her to help him out of both it and his jeans, he'd known enough not to test the limits of his self-control.

She'd watched as he slowly made his way into her bedroom but hadn't followed him into it. He'd been aware of white curtains and an equally white spread, two mismatched dressers and the faint, feminine scent of soap and shampoo that must have come from the adjacent bathroom, and then he'd barely managed to strip down to his briefs before collapsing on the bed. The sheets smelled of her.

He'd like to have convinced himself that his bruises had been responsible for his restlessness during the night, but that wasn't the truth. Not usually a dreamer, he remembered too much of what had gone on inside his mind. Kristen had played the predominant role. Even when his subconscious had insisted on replaying the collision, she'd been standing just outside the arena and the runaway horse had had her eyes. The rest of the time, his dreams had focused entirely on her—and what he wanted and needed from her.

"Joe?"

Struggling to consciousness through his sleep-tangled thoughts, he opened his eyes and looked around until he saw her standing in the doorway.

"I'm sorry. If you're still asleep—"

"No. That's all right." By the amount of light coming in the window, he guessed that it was long after his usual time to get up. The sense of responsibility that had ruled him all his life kicked in, and he sat up and swung his legs over the side. He wasn't as stiff as he thought he'd be although when he touched his left shoulder, he realized that the bruise there went deep.

"It looks pretty bad," she said.

She'd know that only if she'd been studying him. Looking at her again, he noticed that her attention was now on his legs. There was something about wearing only briefs that made him feel more exposed than on the few occasions when he'd worn swim trunks and yet, although she was telling him that she'd prepared breakfast, he cast aside all thoughts of modesty. So she was interested in his legs, was she? Maybe it was time to see how far he could push her—if he didn't fall in with her.

Joe's face, neck, chest, and arms were darker than his legs, but with a little sunlight on them, his entire body had a rich, healthy glow. As it was, the contrast between his tawny skin and her white sheets and spread struck Kristen as both beautiful and right. When he headed into the bathroom, she tried to talk herself into going back to the kitchen, but she was still staring at where he'd spent the night when he rejoined her. He walked even slower this morning, but she wasn't sure if that was because his muscles ached or because he'd felt confined in her small bedroom. His jeans were on the floor. If he had trouble bending over, she'd retrieve them, but she'd much rather he remained dressed—or undressed—the way he was.

"I, ah, I hope you like pancakes," she managed.

"Fine. Kristen, why were you there last night?"

She'd tiptoed around him when she got up this morning, showering quickly and dressing in the bathroom, all the time asking herself what they'd talk about. To avoid anything of a personal nature, she'd intended to question him about the accident, encouraging him to tell her what had happened from his perspective, but with his question, he'd knocked all that from her mind.

"I wanted—" She'd nearly told him that she'd been prompted by Brent's grumbling in the wake of his desire to adopt the boy, but if she did, she'd be lying to herself as well as him. "I wanted to learn more about you," she admitted.

"Why?"

"I'm not sure." She didn't know what to do with her hands, couldn't think how to compose her expression so she wouldn't give away too much. "We saw each other twice last week and each experience was so different."

"We did more than see each other, Kristen. We embraced, kissed."

"Yes. Yes, we did." He hadn't moved from his position at the foot of her bed and yet she almost felt as if he'd reached out and touched her. "But we did more than that," she went on. "You told me things about yourself and I believe I did the same. Those conversations helped me understand you, but it wasn't enough."

"Why not?"

He had no right pushing her! Feeling trapped, she backed away a few steps. "Breakfast is—"

"Breakfast can wait. This can't." To her shock, he held out his hand. "Come here, please."

She did as he ordered, requested, whatever it was. The room had been her sanctuary and security, but now it pulsed with his presence. "Joe, this—"

"This isn't wise. I know."

He still extended his hand, and fool that she was, she took it. Although she knew what Joe was going to do before he pressed her palm against his chest and held it there with his rough fingers, she didn't try to draw away.

"If I'd been after wisdom or what was safe, I wouldn't have let you bring me here last night," he said.

She studied him for a moment. "And I wouldn't have invited you."

"Then we both know what this is about, don't we?"

Joe didn't play games. She'd known that from the start, and what she believed to be his innate honesty had been part of his appeal. She wanted to tell him how afraid she was of letting go, of sharing her body, but he knew about the dark side of her marriage and surely understood that this was hard for her.

"I want you, Kristen," he whispered. "And I believe you want me."

"I . . ."

"Say it."

"I—I want you."

"Good. It's going to be all right." Lifting her hand, Joe covered it with several light kisses before she could feel the loss of his chest's heat. Her legs began to tremble and her ears roared. No matter how many times she blinked, she couldn't see anything except his indistinct outline. "I promise you, it's going to be all right," he whispered.

"I—I'm afraid."

"Of me?"

"No," she admitted.

Her left hand moved almost involuntarily to touch him, sliding over the faint outline of his ribs. He was trembling a little, too.

"Of what?" he pressed. "Just say it, Kristen. What are you afraid of?"

"The past. I don't want it to come back."

"It won't." Releasing her hand, he deftly reached for the top button on her blouse. "I won't let it."

She felt like a half-wild filly on the verge of bolting as he slowly, tenderly removed her blouse and dropped it to the carpet on top of his jeans. She had a brief image of the contrast between soft cotton and worn denim, but that was before he slid a forefinger under her bra.

"We won't talk any more," he whispered. "It's better that way."

He was right, so right because no matter what they might say, it would bring back the world in which she wanted to exist only for and with him.

The slacks she'd put on such a short time ago were quickly unzipped by his capable hands, and she stepped out of them without hesitation. Cliff had insisted on a darkened room before demanding sex, and she'd thought that was the way lovemaking was always conducted, believed her naked body wasn't something a man would want to gaze at, but Joe made no move to draw the curtains. Because the window overlooked the treetops in the small park that was part of the apartment complex, she didn't worry that anyone would see, and even if they had, she wasn't sure that would change anything anyway.

Joe's hands, strong and competent as he went about earning his living, were no less so on Kristen's body. They danced lightly here and there, taking her attention briefly to her shoulders, then her throat, her waist, breasts, the pale skin beneath her panties. Surrounded by him, she thought of rain, the wonder of the precious liquid falling on her, running outside during the infrequent storms and lifting her face so the clouds could drop their bounty on her. Joe's touches were like rain, everywhere, cool and clean, awakening her to the earth's rhythm and her connection with it.

Her own fingers couldn't get enough of him. She

ran them along the muscles in his arms, gentle over his bruised shoulder, reckless and needy when she came to his chest. They had yet to kiss but instead took in every sensation they could through the tips of their fingers. He gave himself up to her, allowed her access to all of him, and although she couldn't yet bring herself to explore what remained protected beneath his briefs, she couldn't get enough of him.

His fingers said she was beautiful. His eyes carried the same message, and she believed him and became strong. Again and again he brushed his palm over her imprisoned breasts until tiny sensations like infant lightning chased over her flesh, heating her and making her head pulse. She began to pant, and each time he teased her erect nipples, she heard herself moan. When, finally, he laid her back on the tangled sheets and cupped his hands over her breasts, she reared up as if to bite him. Ignoring her delicious frustration— either that or showing her the fine line between pain and pleasure—he lowered his head and ran his tongue over what he could reach of the mounded and taut flesh.

It was too much.

"Joe! Please! Please help me!"

He must have known what she needed because he helped her roll onto her side and unfastened her bra. When he pulled it off her with a wild flourish, she settled onto her back again and locked her hands around his neck.

They were sideways on the bed, her legs dangling, his straddling hers and yet despite the impossibility of their position, he managed to slide her panties down over her hips. Feeling trapped by the wisp of clothing, she kicked until it was no longer wrapped around her ankles.

Now it was her turn, and although it meant briefly releasing him, she gave his head freedom, fastened her fingers over the elastic around his hips and yanked downward. Then, wild and wanting, she arched against him, murmuring her need for him over and over.

"Not yet, Kristen," he groaned. "Not yet."

"What—" she started but he was already off her and reaching for his jeans. As he pulled the small foil packet from his wallet, she understood. Eyes closed, body trembling with heat, she waited for him to sheathe himself.

His hands clamped her hips and he easily, deftly slid her around so she was now fully on the bed and although the thick coverlet pressed against the small of her back, she ignored it. Once again, she lifted her hips in primitive invitation.

This time he answered.

THIRTEEN

There was a message from Joe on her voicemail when Kristen got to work Monday morning.

"I'm not good at words," he'd said. "At least not when it comes to what happened Sunday. I just want you to know I'm thinking of you."

Wishing he had said more, needing to hear more, she replayed the message, but it remained just as brief the second time. Although she suspected he was speaking as if someone might overhear, that did nothing to ease the turmoil she felt. They'd finally had the pancake breakfast she'd made for him while they talked about the weather, how much longer it would be until he saw his daughter, the pros and cons of allowing everyone with a horse, regardless of skill level, to enter the Saturday night races, even whether the road department would ever finish working on the street fronting the hospital. Then, finally, he'd asked her to drive him home.

When they had arrived at his place, she'd remained behind the wheel, and Joe had gotten out after thanking her for the lift. Then he'd walked over to her side of the car, leaned in the open window, and kissed her—the kiss going on and on until she thought she was going to fly off into space like a wind-blown leaf.

"It was good," he'd said.

"Yes," she'd replied. "It was."

"And it's going to happen again."

"Joe, I—"

"It is, Kristen. We both know it. What's happening between us is too important for it to be any other way."

Only, she thought as she picked up the first form she had to tend to this morning, she'd been away from him for the better part of twenty-four hours, and although it had been too long returning to her, she'd now regained a measure of her ability to reason.

When she was around Joe, there was simply too much emotion and sensation for her to think straight. She might have been a fool to have brought him home with her the other night and even more of a fool to give him her body, but she was now sitting at her desk and the certificates from the training sessions and workshops she'd attended covered the corkboard above it. She was a social worker, damn it, not some woman on the verge of blindly falling in love.

The morning, as most Mondays were, was insane. She was eating a late lunch of yogurt and a banana at her desk when the day's mail came in. Groaning, she flipped through the current wave of correspondence, stopping only when she came to the next to the last letter. The return address informed her that it was from the State of Nevada Department of Corrections.

Putting down her half-eaten banana, she used a paper clip to open the envelope. There was a single computer generated sheet of paper with Joe's name and social security number at the top. Following that was a brief message. According to their records, Joe had been arrested twice while living there. The first time he'd been charged with reckless driving and resisting arrest. It was the same the second time, only a charge of menacing a police officer had been added, and he'd spent two months in jail and been fined five thousand dollars. In the eyes of the law, Joe Red Shadow was a convicted felon.

Numb, she stared at the words. They blurred, then came into focus, then blurred again. Joe, the man she'd opened her house and life to, slept with, the man she'd thought would provide a parentless boy with security, was a criminal. Had been a criminal, she amended, struggling to remind herself that the events had taken place nearly ten years ago.

But he had warned her, right from the start. *I'm no good for him.*

"Damn it, Joe!" Surging to her feet, she waded up the devastating piece of paper and hurled it at the trash can. "You lied to me!"

Kristen had no real recollection of how she'd gotten out to the construction site. In a distracted way, she knew that she had no business being behind the wheel of a car when she was so angry, but neither could she have remained within the confines of her office cubicle. Following her impulsive outburst, she'd retrieved the incriminating form, straightened it, and brought it with her. Now as she emerged from her vehicle, she held it clutched in her right hand.

There was no sign of Joe, and she wondered if he was even here this afternoon. The thought of having to live with anguish—yes, anguish—trapped inside her made her half-sick. Still, there was nothing she wanted more in life than to turn around and go back where she'd come from.

Kristen finally spotted him in the middle of a group of men and women. Whatever the group was concerned with appeared to be pretty important, judging by their alert stances, heads nodding as they listened to what Joe was saying. Just the same, maybe he sensed her eyes on him because he briefly glanced over his shoulder at her and then fixed her with a longer stare. A couple of minutes later he headed her way.

He was smiling as he approached, the sun warm on his face and his hard hat pushed back to reveal his dark and beautifully alive eyes. When he was close enough to read her expression, his smile faded.

"What is it?" he asked.

He could be so direct with her, honest and open, at least that's what she'd thought. Hadn't he unapologetically told her about taking Brent to see Hannah, making the decision to try to adopt his nephew, letting her know they were going to make love again?

They weren't; everything had changed.

With a trembling hand, she held the rumpled sheet of paper up for him to read. "I got this a few minutes ago," she informed him. If she hadn't learned how to speak and act like a social worker, she wouldn't have been able to continue. "I don't have to tell you what it says, do I?"

If she thought he'd become angry or apologize or accuse her of spying on him, she was mistaken. He simply stood there, his hands at his sides and his dark eyes carving holes in her soul.

"Damn it, Joe, why didn't you tell me?"

"It's history, Kristen."

"Is it?" she challenged. Why hadn't she thought

this through before confronting him. She should have found a way to leave her emotions behind. "I trusted you," she blurted before she could stop herself. "Trusted you to—to be what Brent needs."

"I am."

"No, you're not."

His head snapped back as if she'd slapped him, and despite everything, with all her heart she wanted to apologize for the pain she'd caused him, but he'd hurt her as well.

"What are you saying?" Joe asked through lips that barely moved.

"You're a convicted felon," she managed. The words tasted like poison.

"Was. I've changed in every way that counts."

Was that how he lived with himself, by pretending that that chapter in his life no longer existed? What he had to understand was that her agency wouldn't see it that way.

"Why didn't you tell me?" she repeated.

His body had been ramrod straight, proud and strong, but something in her pain-filled tone must have reached him because he sagged a little, and she sensed rather than saw him start to reach for her. Fortunately for what remained of her sanity, he didn't continue the gesture.

"When I think back to who and what I was then, it makes me sick."

With every fiber in her, she wanted to believe him— did believe. But she had a job to do, a job that left precious little room for what she as a human being and a woman needed out of life.

"So you decided to lie."

"I did not lie!"

For the first time since they'd started talking, his voice rose above a whisper. Kristen realized that they'd attracted considerable attention, but fortunately the others were leaving them alone.

"What do you call it then?" she asked.

"Kristen, I can't change the past, but what counts is who I am today."

"But I don't know who you are!" Her outburst ended in a sob.

"Yes, you do. I'm the man who wants to raise his nephew as if he was his own child. When I've adopted him, you and your agency won't have to worry about him any more. That's what you want, isn't it?"

"Don't talk about adoption, Joe." She hurt so much she wasn't sure she'd survive, but once he fully understood, his wounds would run even deeper. "It's not going to happen."

He jerked and backed away as quickly and surely as if she'd slapped him. "Why not?"

"You say you didn't lie but neither have you been truthful. What do you—"

"Damn it, I will not dredge up what happened back then. It has nothing to do with today."

"In other words, you believe I have no right to know anything about you that you don't want me to know."

"Don't do this. Please, don't do this."

Sometimes her job gave her too much power over people. She'd learned to accept that aspect of it, but it wasn't until today that she hated it. "I know what you're feeling. Believe me, I do. If I had to stand naked in front of some agency, I'd resent it too, but that's the world we live in. You can't select what you're willing or not willing to reveal."

"In other words, I either play the game your way or not at all."

"Not mine. The agency I work for."

He looked on the verge of either shattering or exploding, forcing her to remember that he'd once attacked a police officer, once acted in such an irresponsible way that he'd endangered both himself and those around him. If those instincts still existed in him, she was in serious trouble.

"Even before this," she made herself say, "I had reservations about how things would work out between you and Brent. He resents the fact that you're trying to force your value system on him. He simply wants to be a boy."

"What are you talking about?"

He was right; she wasn't being direct enough. "Your insistence on his embracing an Apache lifestyle. Joe, all he wants is a roof over his head and some stability in his life."

"I've given him that."

Yes, he had, but the reality of his past continued to loom between them. Reaching deep inside herself, she pulled out professionalism and responsibility and left her heart behind to bleed untended.

"I've heard you called wild," she told him. "But it was more than that, wasn't it? What you were convicted of—you have a violent side."

"Had," he hissed. "And it wasn't violence; don't put your personal spin on it. It was self-destruction."

Joe self-destructive? That was incomprehensible and because she'd lived with violence, she clung to that explanation.

"You struck out once, at least once," she said. "And they put you behind bars for it."

"Yes."

"You might lose control again." *The way the man I escaped did.*

"No, I won't."

She had to keep talking because otherwise she'd collapse. "Your telling me that isn't good enough, Joe. Don't you understand?" Although the printout of his record felt as if it weighed a ton, she lifted it so that it appeared like a barrier between them. "This is proof. What I have to go by."

To her shock, he slapped the paper out of her hand. When it fell to the ground, he stepped on it.

"What happens now?" he asked, his voice thick with emotion.

Although he didn't say more than those few words, she knew exactly what he was asking—knew and hated herself for what was coming next. "I can't allow Brent to go on living with you."

His muscles gathered and for an instant she wondered if he was going to strike her. Just the same, she didn't back away but stood where she was as emotion poured out of him—out of both of them. A few precious and innocent hours ago, she'd wondered if she was falling in love with him. Now she knew the journey had indeed begun—and it made this confrontation even more devastating.

Dragging her gaze off the crushed paper, she forced herself to meet Joe's eyes. They looked so terribly old, determined and beaten at the same time. Strength still radiated from him, but he'd become a corralled horse with no way of regaining his freedom.

I'm sorry, Joe. Sorry for both of us. She couldn't voice the words.

The realization of the hollowness she felt came before she fully understood that Joe had turned from her and was stalking toward the unfinished structure he was responsible for. Reaching the foundation, he signaled to the man working the crane that he wanted to be lifted. The massive hook swung down, and he stopped it in the middle of an arc, straddled the hook and held on until he reached the division between the first and second floor. Then, although the hook continued to sway a little, he scrambled off and onto a parallel support beam.

He seemed to be having trouble with his balance and gripped the nearest vertical beam with his left hand in order to support himself. As he was doing so, the hook swung toward him. He ducked and crouched at the same time.

Kristen watched with her breath caught in her throat, her heart crying and her body lonely. To call Joe wild wasn't an accusation but a compliment. She only needed to look at him now to know that with every fiber of her being. She was still watching him, still capturing this moment so it might sustain her for the rest of her life, when Joe's left arm, deeply bruised from his accident Saturday night, failed him.

Graceful, almost accepting, he slipped off the beam and fell to the ground.

Hours after Joe had been admitted to the hospital, Kristen was finally allowed in to see him. By then she'd learned that in addition to a couple of broken ribs and contusions that put his earlier ones to shame, he'd sustained a concussion and a bruised kidney. The attending emergency room physician made it clear that he'd have to spend the night there for observation.

Fortunately, he'd make a full recovery—at least physically.

When she first stepped into the room, she thought he was asleep, but she was slowly walking toward him, her heart hammering, when his eyes opened and he focused on her.

"I didn't know if you'd be here," he said, his voice slightly slurred.

"You didn't—" she began but couldn't finish. The pain in his eyes tore her apart, not just because she hated seeing him in physical pain, but because she knew what he felt went far deeper than that. Unable to stop herself, she took his hand. To her relief, it felt neither hot or cold. Remembering how he'd kissed her palm, it was all she could do not to give him the same, but everything between them had fallen apart in one shattering day. Yet she refused to say it might be over for them.

"I'm sorry," Kristen whispered even though they were, at least briefly, alone. "So sorry this happened."

"It isn't your fault."

She didn't agree, but what would arguing with him prove? Because she didn't know what else to say, she told Joe that his entire crew had wanted to follow the ambulance. When they'd been discouraged, they'd remained at work but had swamped the hospital switchboard with their calls.

"What about Brent?" he asked. His eyes reminded her of glowing embers.

"He's in the waiting room. With Susanna. I—I asked if I could see you first."

"Why?"

She'd known he'd ask her that and should have prepared an answer but seeing him alive left room for nothing else inside her. Instead of acknowledging his question, she tried to make herself release his hand. Failing that, she lifted it so she could concentrate on the outline of bones and veins, the muscles roping his arm.

"I was so afraid," she admitted.

"I don't think I had time for that. I can't remember everything."

"You were trying to get out of the way of that hook when you lost your balance or something."

"I don't lose my balance, not if I'm paying attention."

"You couldn't have been. The things we'd said to each other—"

"I don't want to talk about that now."

Joe's stoic silence, his self-protective shield, had brought them to this awful place in their relationship—was destroying it—but at this moment, she loved him too much to tell him that.

"What *do* you want to talk about?" she asked.

"You. Us." He glanced at the closed door behind her. "Is anyone going to come barging in?"

"I don't know. I hope not."

His features tightened, then became unreadable. "I don't think I lost consciousness for long," he said. "I remember people gathering around me and then the ambulance coming and the ride here. You were beside me right after I fell; I remember that."

"Yes."

"But you weren't in the ambulance and not in the emergency room."

"I—they wouldn't let me in while they were working on you."

"But you came."

"Yes." It seemed as if waiting for word of his condition had taken forever.

"Why?"

She couldn't shy away from this penetrating question, and had known that he would ask it sooner or later.

"Joe?" Hoping for a small measure of calm, Kristen took a deep breath. "If you'd died today, I think I would have died with you."

"I'm that important to you?"

If some part of her nature needed to hold back from that revelation, the voice was too small for her to heed it. "You're that important to me," she admitted.

"Do you love me?"

Yes. "I—I don't know. Maybe."

He stared at her for a moment, then closed his eyes. His fingers continued to return her grip.

"You wouldn't have liked me a few years ago," Joe said after a brief silence. "I sure as hell didn't."

When he didn't immediately continue, she nearly prompted him, but whatever he told her would have to be given willingly.

"I thought I could pretend I'd been reborn after my conviction, that I could walk away from everything, but I was wrong. You made that clear."

"Joe, I—"

"Don't. It's my turn to talk; I have no choice. Kristen, I was barely eighteen when my daughter was born." Opening his eyes, he held them steady on hers. "Throughout Marci's pregnancy, I told myself it wasn't happening, that I wasn't ready to become a father and that the birth wouldn't change anything. I drove her to the hospital and saw April being born, but for too much of it, I just wasn't there. I'm not proud of that, but it's the truth."

The truth.

"So much changed the first time I saw my daughter," Joe whispered. "When I first held her in my arms."

Throat burning, she nodded, guessing he knew it had been the same for her when Susanna was born.

There was a ragged catch to his breath that she sensed had nothing to do with his injuries. "Before that, I was a high school dropout, working dead-end jobs, running around and doing stupid, destructive things because nothing mattered."

"Your parents—"

"My dad was drunk most of the time. My mother was sixteen when I was born and they left me with relatives most of the time. I hadn't seen or spoken to them for over a year when April was born, had barely acknowledged my parents since I entered my teens."

Because she'd seen too many rootless, throwaway kids, she knew what Joe was talking about. She wanted to compliment him on his current relationship with his father, but that could wait.

"I wanted to be a father for April, but I didn't know how."

Oh, Joe. "Because you'd had no role model."

"Maybe. It doesn't matter. I could barely support myself and had nothing to offer Marci and we knew it'd be a disaster if we got married. I didn't object when she took April and left Nevada to live with her parents again. Not seeing my daughter . . ." His eyes glistened. "I was so alone . . . that's when I got into trouble with the law."

She'd lifted Joe's hand to her mouth without being aware of it, and she didn't try to stop herself from kissing the tips of his fingers. If he could sense her shaking or feel her unshed tears, so be it.

He swallowed and took a deep breath. "I couldn't sleep. Every time I tried, an image of my daughter would form in my mind and my arms would ache."

"Oh, Joe."

"So I stopped sleeping and filled every hour with activity. Drank like my father, and did every self-destructive, crazy thing I could—just to kill the pain inside."

His eyes glazed, but she made no attempt to pull him back to her. The memories he was dredging up couldn't be shared, had to be experienced all over again.

"The first time they put me in jail, I was so out of it I still don't remember everything," he admitted, his voice husky. "What I do remember is sobering up and feeling as if I'd been thrown into a dungeon. I swore I'd never let that happen again, never look at the world through bars again, but I was wrong."

When his words fell away this time, Kristen still gave no thought to prompting him to continue. Instead, she tried to envision his capable hands wrapped around the steel bars that kept him prisoner and understood as she hadn't before how vital it was for him to close that chapter on his past.

"I didn't learn," he said. "I drank again but even when I wasn't drunk, I couldn't stop the nightmares. The self-hate."

"Because of April?"

He nodded. "She deserved so much, but I was even more useless as a parent than mine had been. The second time I got arrested—I lost it."

"Tell me."

His hands, always before steady and strong, now shook a little. "The time I spent paying for what I'd done was both the worst and best thing that could have happened to me. I decided that, no matter what I did with the rest of my life, this would not be how my daughter remembered me."

Her eyes burned but she made no attempt to stop her tears. If there was a world beyond the two of them here in the hospital room, she had no awareness of it.

"Kristen, my daughter was my salvation."

Unable to speak, she nodded.

"My redemption. I'm no longer the man—the idiot—I was when those things happened in Nevada. I was estranged from my people, but somehow I knew I had to get back to them if I was going to hold it all together. Learning about my heritage gave me roots." He sucked in air. "That's why I want what I do for Brent."

She nearly asked why he hadn't told her that before, but his tone and the look in his eyes supplied the answer. He'd truly been reborn while in jail and unable to escape reality. Determined to turn his life around, Joe had done just that but that didn't make talking about the mistakes of the past any easier—especially not to her.

"How much does April know?"

"As much as she's capable of understanding. I'll tell her the whole story once she's old enough."

Because April was his daughter, his love and life while, she, Kristen—

No! She refused to do that to herself, to them.

Joe's eyes were asking what was going to happen now, but her heart's answer couldn't be expressed in words. Instead of trying, she leaned over him and touched her lips to his. The first time they'd kissed, their interlocked hands had created a barrier between them, but because she no longer wanted or needed that, she released his hands so she could run her fingers into his hair. As she lost herself in the hunger and need and fulfillment of their kiss, she felt his fingers on her back.

This man, this strong and complex man, had bared his deepest secrets to her and what had been a flicker of love burst to life. Kristen knew in her heart of hearts that she'd been changed by him forever.

I love you, she mouthed with her lips pressed against his.

"What did you say?" he asked.

"I—that I love you."

"After everything I told you?"

"Because of that. Joe, you're the bravest, most honest man I know."

"It wasn't easy."

"I know," she said, laughing a little. "It took falling off a building for you to finish the telling."

"Just like it took Susanna being in danger for you to discover how strong and brave you are." He trailed his fingers over her throat. "I love you, Kristen. That's what I was thinking when that hook was heading for me. How much I love you, and that I was going to have to climb back down and tell you everything and take my chances. I guess it took falling off a building to knock some sense into me."

Not sure whether she was laughing or crying, she nodded.

"Kristen, what happens now?"

Although they were inside, it felt as if the two of

them were floating through the sky towards a horizon that went on forever. "Now we work together," she whispered. "For Brent's future and yours."

"And for ours," he told her.

They were gazing into each other's eyes when the door opened and she heard footsteps. Looking up but still stroking Joe's hair, she acknowledged Brent and her daughter. The two stood hand in hand, their wide eyes taking in the unfamiliar sight of Joe laid low. Proudly displayed on Brent's chest was his eagle feather necklace.

EPILOGUE

Kristen walked up behind Joe, wrapped her arms around his waist, and looked over his shoulder at the two youngsters engaged in grooming a half-grown foal. Perhaps by unspoken agreement, Brent tended to the animal's back and withers while Susanna was busily running her brush over the youngster's legs. Shirtless because of the heat, Brent nevertheless still wore the eagle feather he'd put on in the hospital. Although he took it off when he showered, he'd proudly displayed it ever since that afternoon.

"They work well together," Joe observed. "Maybe we'll be able to hire them out as a pair at the local stable."

"Only as long as we get a cut. After all, we're the ones feeding them."

"Good point." Reaching around, he drew her to his side, holding her tight against him. "One night in a hospital will last me for the rest of my life. I can't believe how much I missed seeing the sun."

The sun was indeed worth more than a casual look today, but she could wait to do that. Joe had been out of the hospital the better part of a week but was still expressing gratitude for his freedom. She, however, had much more than that to be thankful for. They both did.

"You were so convincing today," she told him. "I didn't know what to expect from the tribal council, surely not that they'd make such a quick decision."

"I didn't say that much, just how I feel about Brent," Joe said. "Having him there to say he'd run away if they tried to place him anywhere else carried a lot of weight, but you're the one who did the rest. I'm grateful to you, so grateful."

On this peaceful Saturday afternoon, the last thing she wanted to talk about was anything to do with work. If she had her way, the hours until the children were in bed would quickly fade away, and she and Joe would be in each other's arms once more. However, she understood that Joe needed to talk about what had happened, make it real for himself.

"I presented them with my observations, that's all," she said.

"Observations don't come with emotion; what you told them did. You said you had no doubts about my ability to be the father figure Brent needs. And that the most important thing I'd be giving him was love."

"Because that's what I believe."

"It wasn't that way very long ago."

"No, it wasn't," she admitted. "Joe, I want to put that behind us. I understand how hard it was for you to admit what you were like back then, and you're right; it's history. Today is what matters."

"Yes, it is."

After that, neither of them seemed to have anything to say, allowing her to lose herself in emotion. Not only had Brent pleaded to continue living with his uncle, but he'd concluded by saying that nearly losing

Joe had brought home how much he loved and needed him. Joe had been right, he'd said. Without someone to belong to, without a past and a heritage, there wasn't much to look forward to.

Content to stand with Joe's arm around her, she was slow to realize that he'd taken her hand and was closing it around his own eagle feather.

"You have an Apache heart," he whispered, his breath against the side of her neck. "And because you do, you should have an Apache name."

"I-I'd like that."

"Would you?" Bending down, he kissed her temple. "How does Gentle Wind sound?"

"Gentle Wind? I love it. Was she in the legends?"

"Don't you remember? From the legends? Kristen, Gentle Wind was the first Red Shadow wife."

"Oh."

He pulled her closer and looked into her eyes. "Do you know what that means?"

She shook her head, although she knew instinctively what he was trying to say. Still, the pleasure of hearing the words from his lips was worth pretending ignorance. Joe cleared his throat and took a deep breath.

"I want you to be mine. Forever. Will you marry me?"

Kristen said yes with a kiss that neither of them would ever forget.